Addicted

TO A DETROIT
SAVAGE

A Novel By

APRIL NICOLE

ACKNOWLEDGMENTS

I want to thank God, first and foremost, for this amazing opportunity to allow my dreams to come true. I also want to thank my supporters, Anthony B., Yolanda F., Pernail D. and Taliea W. for reading my rough drafts and giving me constructive criticism to help strengthen my work. You guys have all put in countless hours to read my million and one rough drafts. Finally, my daughter Aiyana Nicole, I did this for you so we can make it out the hood together. Please forgive me if I have forgotten anyone.

Momma I made it, POPs hold it down, rest peacefully.

−Love, April Nicole Marie

Cut the bullshit. Let's get started, shall we?
  -Kairo

THE BEGINNING

BEEP BEEEEP BEEP!! This cold particular morning, Kairo jumped up out her sleep as she awoke to the familiar sounds of a tow truck, towing someone's car.

"Shit! I hope they are not towing my truck outside. I know I missed a couple of payments, but damn. Can a sister get a warning first?" she said to herself as she immediately rushed over to the window being nosy, praying to God it wasn't her truck. Lo and behold, it was her truck that was being towed. "Hold the fuck up, I got money right here!" she yelled, grabbing the crumpled hundreds off the dining room table.

She didn't have much but gave what she could. Kairo was struggling trying to make ends meet, not trying to depend on her parents all the time. How did she look? A grown ass woman calling to ask her parents for money. Fuuuck that, she had too much pride for that. She would rather sell her ass before she called them. She didn't have time to hear them give her the third degree about how she should have finished college.

Rushing, Kairo breezed right past the eviction notice that was taped on her door. Finally making it outside, she waved at the towing man. By this time, her 2020 Range was already loaded onto the flat bed on the back of his truck.

"Sir, I have the money for this week's payment right here!" Kairo said gasping for air, trying to catch her breath. She sounded like a fat bitch running from the police. As she got closer to the very attractive man, she could feel her stomach turning knots. Just as it did when she saw any other fine ass man. He was handsome, and she wasn't exactly dressed to flirt to get herself out of this situation.

After all, she had on a granny robe, some gym shoes and a black hair bonnet. Looking like she was straight out of these projects. He was standing tall at 6ft with a low-cut fade with deep 360 waves. His teeth were so damn white you would think he brushed them with bleach.

"Ma'am, I'm sorry, but you should have paid your note on time. I have been authorized to tow your truck, not to take payments," he replied nonchalantly. "You should make your payments on time and I wouldn't even be here."

Kairo's heart felt like it skipped a beat or two. *Oh no the fuck he didn't just go there.* She looked for his name and spotted it on the left side of his chest. He didn't even look like a damn Tyrone. *Who the fuck would name him that?* she thought.

"Excuse me, Mr. Asshole, you don't have to be so damn rude about it," she uttered with an attitude, throwing the money at him. He turned and looked at Kairo like she was crazy. Then he proceeded walking back to the truck. She was running out of time; it was either she called her parents, or she sell that ass. Oh well, fuck it. She didn't have time to think. Kairo said the first thing that came to her mind.

"Ok wait, I apologize. How about I suck your dick then?" she offered, grabbing his strong, muscular arm hoping this would work. He didn't even budge not even a little bit. He slammed the truck door in her face and then pulled off. Kairo could feel the blood rushing to her face, as she just made an ass out of herself. That hurt her pride, watching her brand-new 2020 Black Range Rover being hauled away.

"FUCK YOU, YO' BALLS PROBABLY STANK ANYWAY, YOU MOTHERFUCKER!!!!" Kairo screamed at the top of her lungs causing attention to fall on her in the middle of the street. She didn't give a damn who heard or saw her. For one, it was too early for the bullshit and for two, he had her fucked up. She really wasn't going to suck his dick, she just thought it sounded good. Desperate times called for desperate measures, but she still wouldn't suck his dick even if he was the last man standing on earth.

All the neighbors were now standing in their windows watching her. She bet their ole nosey asses were having a field day watching miss goody two shoes throw her pride down the drain. A very embarrassed Kairo headed back to her condo. "The fuck y'all looking at?" she asked, snatching the eviction notice down.

"Bitch, your broke ass!" the woman whose condo was adjacent from Kairo's mumbled, before slamming the door. Kairo just ignored her and continued to go inside her home; she had other things to worry about besides some woman that probably was just broke as her. She didn't have time for the extra shit, she wanted her truck back.

"I swear you can't do shit in Detroit without the next motherfucka knowing about it. Your business be spread through the city like a wildfire. Everybody and they momma know your business but rather talk shit than help their own people," Kairo mumbled to herself while calling Cali for a ride. She was still avoiding calling her parents for help, because she knew she hadn't talked to them in over a year.

Kairo was the youngest of seven siblings and one of the realest females you could ever meet on the Eastside of Detroit. She kept things real, never had to sugar coat a damn thing and wasn't ashamed to go for what she knew. Even if it meant she couldn't get what she needed to get. Although she never sold her ass before, she had no problem testing the waters. Everybody in the hood knew Kairo because of her parents. They were famous pastors over two megachurches called Spiritual Word of Faith Ministries located on the East and West side of Detroit. That was how Kairo acquired her expensive taste in clothes, cars and jewelry, living through her parents.

Kairo was their favorite because she was their last miracle, so she never had responsibilities as far as paying bills, because they always paid them for her. Long as she stayed in college to earn her doctorate degree, but Kairo dropped out after her fourth year. She no longer wanted to be a doctor but a registered nurse instead. The decision she made disappointed her parents causing them to cut her off completely. Her bank account was tapped within two weeks after her parents stopped giving her monthly allowances. Now she was struggling to maintain her fancy life as well as her bills.

HOOOONK!!! Cali pulled up 30 minutes later, blowing her horn and blasting "Act Up" by City Girls. Kairo just knew that was Cali's ghetto ass. You could hear her car a mile away, it was just that loud. California, "Cali," was Kairo's friend. They met a couple summers back in college after discovering they had so much in common. Looking at her, you would never know she had four children, she didn't look like she ever ate. Cali was a short, petite woman with long brown hair who often got attention because of her light skin and hazel eyes.

"Come on bitch, you know some of us want to get to work on time!" Cali yelled, honking her horn two more times. Before Kairo could even step one foot into the car, she blew her horn again. This irritated Kairo because Cali already gave her the vibe she didn't want to pick her up.

"Okay, damn, can I get in first?" Kairo asked, irritated. Cali was acting all impatient and shit like she had other things to do. Cali never was the type to really speak her mind.

"Kairo, it took you ten years to get down the stairs, and finally into the car." Cali huffed, pressing hard on the gas. She had this funky ass attitude as if she didn't want to be bothered with Kairo.

"Well what the fuck is wrong with you?" Kairo questioned her, because Cali was mad. It took Cali literally five minutes before she decided to reply.

"Nothing, I just don't understand why I had to come all the way East, when you know I have no gas money!" Cali sucked her teeth, yelling at Kairo, like she wasn't in the same car sitting right next to her.

"Ok, something is seriously wrong with you, because you yelling at me like I'm one of your kids. Damn, I got my truck repossessed. Can you have some compassion?" Kairo asked, rolling the window down to avoid the cigarette smoke because Cali had her car filled with it. Kairo didn't smoke cigarettes so it made her feel uncomfortable, cigarettes stank and tasted funny.

"That's your damn fault," Cali paused taking a long puff of her cigarette, "you could have hopped your happy ass right on the DDOT, Gratiot bus to Eight mile. Don't nobody have time for this."

"Excuse me, no the fuck you didn't just say that," Kairo was shocked Cali would even say that dumb shit. She knew it was true, it was Kairo's own fault her truck got repossessed. But Kairo was more shocked Cali would even suggest that she catch the damn bus. As many times as Kairo traveled around for her and her nappy headed ass kids, not asking for a damn dime for gas, she could have at least returned the favor.

"Well I'm just saying Kairo, you need—"

"Shut the fuck up Cali," Kairo snapped, cutting her off. "You sound goofy as fuck right now. I had the money and he didn't want to take it."

"Girl, sounds like you're in some deep shit, trying to keep up with the joneses," she hinted, blowing her smoke in Kairo's direction. Cali really was tempting Kairo to smack her since she knew the smell of cigarettes made Kairo nauseous.

"Really bitch?" Kairo said, smacking her lips and shifting her body towards Cali. This girl was acting funny as fuck towards her. Kairo didn't understand what this was all about, and she wasn't about to play 21 clues to find out either.

"What?" Cali paused before continuing her insults, "Well you're the one living above your means. Don't get mad at me because you don't pay your damn bills on time."

"No, Cali, you started this shit, sounding stupid as fuck. Suggesting I catch the bus and shit. Who the fuck wants to catch the DDOT when I'm the only one in Detroit sporting a 2020 Range?" Kairo's voice was now getting hostile because Cali was now pissing her off. Cali was trying to pull her hoe card; she was acting funny towards her for no reason. Even Stevie Wonder could see the bullshit, and he was blind.

If she didn't want me to catch a ride with her, I would have caught a Lyft or Uber. All she had to do was communicate, I'm no fucking psychic. How was I supposed to know she didn't have gas in her car? Kairo thought to herself. The more she pondered on her suggesting she catch the bus, the more she got distressed.

"Pull over, I'll Uber the rest of the way," Kairo implied, finally having enough of Cali's stinking cigarette and her talking shit.

"Are you serious right now?" Cali had a sour expression on her face.

"Yea, you are acting goofy for no reason, doing the fucking most!" Kairo got out, slamming Cali's raggedy ass car door.

"Oh come on, with your sensitive ass. Don't be stupid!" Cali yelled back, putting the car in park in the middle of Gratiot.

"Fuck you California, I don't have time for this shit!" Kairo was mad, arguing with her over gas money.

"Ok, Kairo, I apologize. Can you get back into the car before we both get fired?" Cali begged.

Kairo was still mad at that pickle head ass bitch. Only reason why she got back into the car was because she needed a ride to work. Otherwise, Kairo would have two footed her ass all the way to Eight Mile, not caring about how far she had to walk. Just as long as she wasn't in the same car as Cali. After ten minutes of silence, Cali finally broke the awkwardness.

"I got some wood and Runts in the glove compartment if you want to fire it up before we start our shift," she said, kissing Kairo's ass now trying to be nice.

"Nah, I'm straight," Kairo politely declined and continued to stare out the window at the rain that was now pouring hard, making it impossible to see.

"Since when Kairo, the stoner of this age, passes up on a wood?" Cali looked at Kairo surprised because she was not used to her not smoking dank with her.

"I don't have time for your shit today. I just want to get to work please," Kairo murmured, still holding a grudge against Cali, turning her body away to face the window. She finally got the hint that Kairo wasn't joking around with her and she remained quiet for the rest of the ride.

Pulling up to Papa's Diner, Kairo spotted the same tow truck with her Range on the flat bed. It was parked on the side of Marbud Ave off Eight Mile. Kairo's body temperature shot through the roof. She was damn near a ticking time bomb ready to explode any minute now. She was embarrassed because everyone knew she was the only person in Detroit with a 2020 Range Rover. If anybody saw her, it was TJ's nosy ass pulling up at the same time as Cali. He parked right next to them rushing to get out to talk shit.

"Giiiirrrllll, I know that's not your whip in the back of that tow truck?" TJ said, placing one of his hands on his hip and snapping his fingers together with the other. TJ was very flamboyant and he was one of the nosiest motherfuckas you could ever meet. He knew the whole world's business and he only lived in Detroit. Kairo swore his gay ass needed a show all by himself.

"Dayyum TJ, you got a lot of white shit on your nose. When did you start doing coke before your shift starts?" Kairo questioned in a sarcastic tone. He knew where she was going with it and he needed to mind his own business.

TJ pointed his boney finger at Kairo. "What bitch? Now you are tweakin'," he chortled, walking into the diner. Tyrone was sitting in the corner booth alone drinking coffee, Kairo assumed. TJ began to draw attention to himself talking loudly while Cali went straight to go clock in.

"Well damn, he is fine as hell, mmmm," TJ said and licked his lips together. "He looks like Omari Hardwick in a repo man suit, Happy Halloween!"

"Maybe he will let you suck his dick then, since I was turned down," Kairo said, rushing past TJ so she could avoid eye contact with Tyrone, but it was too late; he already saw her. He looked at Kairo as if he knew who she was already, staring at her from head to toe. Their eyes locked and had been staring at each other for more than two minutes. Kairo could feel her blood boiling underneath her skin, suddenly remembering she was at work. She got mad all over again, flipping the finger at him and continued to go in the back.

"OOOOHH chiiillleee! If you don't hurry up and get your truck back," TJ said, handing Kairo her apron.

"TJ, first she needs to get her shit together," Cali chimed in, rolling her eyes. Before Kairo knew it, she leaped in Cali's face, about to slap the shit out of her. Wasn't nobody even talking to Cali, and she'd been attacking Kairo all morning. She didn't know what the fuck her problem was.

"Chill on me Cali, you worried about me you need to get your kids out the system. Before I slap the cowboy shit out of you," Kairo threatened her, pointing out Cali's failure because all her children were taken. Kairo removed herself out the kitchen before Cali could respond and she got fired for slapping a bitch. Kairo walked towards the front to start collecting orders, and Delano was now sitting at the counter waiting for her to come out. She tried to walk past without looking at him.

"Excuse me Kairo!" he said, trying to get her attention. Kairo kept walking like she didn't hear him. Then she felt his strong hand on her shoulder. "I'm not gone beg for your attention"—he put both of his hands in the air surrendering—"just want to talk to you really quick."

"What's up? Because you are distracting me from my money," Kairo said with an attitude, rolling her eyes and smacking her lips.

Delano then proceeded to say, "I see you need extra cash, and working here you won't be able to afford those payments on that truck and your condo." Kairo looked at him like he was fucking crazy. *Where does he get off saying shit like that?* she thought to herself.

"So, you think you know me?" Kairo asked, crossing both of her arms over her chest.

"Actually, I do, but what's with this attitude? I'm trying to help you, relax," he replied, taking a sip of his coffee.

"Seriously, so now you trying to help me?" Kairo questioned, fanning her right hand. "Can you give me my fucking truck back?"

"Kairo, do you want to know what it is or not?" Delano asked, now getting irritated by how carelessly she acted.

"Fuck you, give me back my fucking truck!" Kairo stood up trying to leave, then he forced her to sit back down with his strong Arm and Hammer ass.

"Don't you know you could come up missing if you don't pay Johnny his money on time?" Delano claimed, still looking around to see if someone was watching them.

"Who the fuck is Johnny?" Kairo contested, snatching her arm away, getting up from the table, causing people in the diner to gasp. Hoping he wasn't expecting her to listen to that bullshit, because he was talking crazy, she couldn't even take him seriously. How dare he say he knew her. She ain't never seen that man a day in her life, at least that's what she thought.

"Kairo, can you join me in my office please?" Mr. Banks signaled her to follow him, finally rescuing her from that crazy man. She rolled her eyes and sucked her teeth.

"I wonder what the fuck this about now," she uttered to herself. When she entered the room, Cali was leaving abruptly. She thought to herself, *what the fuck is going on?* Maybe she might have snitched about what took place earlier.

"Yes, Mr. Banks?" Kairo said in her most innocent voice. She wasn't prepared for what was about to come next.

"Kairo, I value you as an employee, but I'm a have to let you go," Mr. Banks said, looking towards the ground.

"Hold up, why are you firing me?" she argued, because she really wanted to know if it was Cali that snitched on her. Although Cali did snitch on her, Mr. Banks wasn't going to tell her that.

"I don't have to say, but termination is effective immediately." Mr. Banks held his head down, opening the door for Kairo to leave.

"Oh yea, well fuck you too, you shrimp dick fuck!!!!" she screamed as she was leaving out his office. Kairo knew that Mr. Banks would show favoritism between her and Cali because they were fucking on the low. Cali used to share all the details with Kairo when they first started messing around.

"Fuck this job!!" Kairo said, throwing her apron down on the ground and heading outside. As soon as she stepped outside, the rain started pouring down again. "FUCK MY LIFE!!!" she cried, as her clothes and hair were now soaked from the rain. Delano watched Kairo as she stomped and pouted as the rain fell heavily onto her head. He figured this would be the perfect opportunity to catch her alone. So, he quietly exited the diner, leaving a stack of flyers to his grand opening tonight on the counter.

"Do you need a ride?" Delano asked, running after Kairo with a black umbrella. Kairo looked back to see who was approaching her. She was so embarrassed from what just happened, she accepted his offer without putting up a fight. Delano, being a gentleman, gave Kairo his umbrella and assisted her inside the truck. "I'm Delano by the way," he extended his hand out for a handshake. "Don't mind the uniform, it's my coworker's."

"Wait, so your name is not Tyrone?" she asked. Kairo was confused as to why he would wear another man's uniform instead of his own. At first Delano hesitated, to make sure she was serious, and stared at her before responding.

"Fuck no! Do I look like a Tyrone?" He chuckled, flashing his perfectly white teeth again. He knew he struck for gold when his plan was falling into place. After he spent many countless nights on this moment, he didn't know how he was going to approach her.

"Well it's nice to meet you, I'm Kairo," she extended her hand back for him to shake. She was unaware Delano was no stranger. He was indeed someone from her childhood. She just couldn't tell by his facial hair and his muscular arms.

"Oh, I know exactly who you are, no need for an introduction," he said, looking at her seductively licking his bottom lip. Kairo was beautiful even though she was drenched from the rain.

"You don't know shit about me, so why do you think you know me?" she yelled at Delano, offended. Kairo had an attitude because he kept saying he knew her, but not telling her how he knew her. So, she folded her arms across her chest.

"Now, you are being a brat. Should I just be quiet while driving you home?" Delano asked, coming to a stop at the red light. She figured she could be nice to the man; after all, he was kind enough to take her home.

"No, I apologize. I'm just having a bad day as you can see," Kairo was looking out the window staring at the heavy rain that pelted against the streets. This was one nasty storm on a Friday evening, the sounds of thunder soaring throughout the sky. It was growing dark outside so the streetlights came on earlier than usual.

"Yea, I see, shit has been rough for you, but all I'm doing is trying to offer my help. What's the matter, you not used to people helping you?" Delano asked, turning South on Gratiot towards Downtown. Kairo's pride was just as big as her ego, but that was something she needed to work on. She was so used to getting her way, from her parents and all seven siblings. She was downright spoiled, rotten to the fucking core.

"That's cool, you can drop me off here, and I can walk the rest of the way," Kairo insisted, ignoring the question that Delano just asked her. She was frustrated and didn't want him to know she depended on her parents for everything. Although he already knew much about her, she just didn't know how much he knew.

"You sure?" he asked. "It's bad out there, all that raining, thundering and lightning." He was trying to persuade Kairo to stay inside, but Kairo was stubborn and rebellious; that was just how she was. That didn't make Delano change the way he felt about her. He still loved her regardless of how stubborn she could be.

"I'll take my chances, a little rain not gone hurt anybody," Kairo retorted, rushing to get out while the truck was still in motion. Soon as she opened the door, Delano grabbed her arm to prevent her from falling out the truck. If he would have never done so, things would have ended badly for her.

"Stop! Here, you can have these back." Delano handed her the keys to the truck. He didn't want to see Kairo walking in the cold, dark streets in the rain. Especially not on the Eastside of Detroit, it was dangerous on this side of town. After all, he already served his purpose of taking the truck. Which was remove the tracking device and getting Kairo's attention.

"Wait, what are you doing?" Kairo asked, confused. "Isn't Johnny or whatever his name is gone come after me?"

"Not if I already paid the bill, and I also paid your rent up three months in advance," Delano replied, as he was unloading the truck removing the straps around the wheels. The chains clinked together as the truck was being released from the towing bed.

"When did you do this? Because I'm not fucking you," she asked, shocked. She never knew any man to pay her bills. They would buy her Dolce and Gabbana purses, Louboutin pumps, you know, materialistic shit, but never paid her bills. She tried to remain calm, but she really was excited someone had shown some kindness to her. She was relieved she didn't have to call her parents after all.

"No girl, I can't show a little compassion? Besides, this happened right when you got fired," Delano lied. He already paid the note a month ahead he just hid his intentions. Johnny set a death bounty on her head because she missed a few payments, but he wasn't going to lay a finger on her. He was happy to finally be in Kairo's presence after searching for her for over ten years.

"Wait, this doesn't make sense. How do you even know that?" She laughed because she was embarrassed. She couldn't believe what she was hearing. He knew too much about her, and now she was beginning to wonder who he was. "Who the fuck are you, the feds?" Kairo asked, leaning up in her seat to get a better view of Delano's face.

"Girl, I'm not your enemy here. Why don't you meet me here tonight?" Delano handed her a black velvet business card with an address. Tonight was Delano's grand opening to the hottest strip club in the city.

"Um, what is this for?" she inquired, frustrated because nothing was making sense.

"Meet me there Kairo. I promise to tell you everything tonight," he said before he pulled off, leaving her there at the train tracks in the middle of Gratiot right before French Rd.

Ring! Ring!

As soon as Kairo climbed into her truck, her phone began to ring.

"What's good Cali?" Kairo answered coolly into the phone receiver.

"So, I got to ask this question, did you tell Don about Mr. Banks and I?" Cali asked harshly, her business was exposed moments after Kairo walked out the door. Kairo looked at the phone and said, "Bitch what? Now why the fuck would I do that?"

"Did you, or did you not call him?" Cali asked with an attitude. Loud noise was in the background from Mr. Banks and Don fighting.

"Cali, why the fuck would I call your man? That's your man, don't be testing me for my loyalty. Bitch, you're the one that needs to be questioned," Kairo snapped.

"All I'm saying is Don found out, and you're the only one that knows about Mr. Banks and me. Now, they're both up here fighting and blood is leaking everywhere.

"Well what do you want me to do Cali? I just got fired and here you are calling me with this bullshit." Kairo rolled her eyes. *Her friend,* she thought, was now checking her.

"You know what, I apologize. How about we talk about this at your place?" Cali suggested. She knew she was wrong for accusing Kairo of talking to Don.

"Yea, that's fine. I guess we can do that," Kairo said before hanging up the phone. She was always down for a conversation, and maybe she could find out why Cali was being a bitch today. *Maybe she is on the rag or something,* Kairo thought to herself as she pulled off and headed home.

Although they both collided heads earlier, Kairo forgave Cali as if nothing happened. She knew where her help came from. Kairo was the only person she could really talk to about anything. They might not always see eye to eye, but no friendship was made perfect nor was it made to last.

KAIRO WAS near her home before she stopped by the liquor store to get some wine. She just couldn't stop thinking about Delano. He was handsome, but knew too much about her and she needed to find out how. This piqued her curiosity and she suspected he wanted something, or maybe he was interested in her. Kairo remembered one thing she learned from her brothers, *if a man is truly interested in you, he will do anything and everything necessary to get your attention.* Kairo giggled at the thought and proceeded to go home.

Kairo pulled up, and Cali was there pulling her bags out the trunk. She was confused, because she said talk, not move in with her. *Whatever*, Kairo scoffed, thinking to herself, and helped Cali with her luggage.

"Girl I thought you said we were going to talk?" Kairo asked, but Cali ignored her.

"Bitch, we got to go out tonight. I'm a whole ass single woman na," Cali said, struggling with her bag of clothes she was carrying up the stairs.

"Damn, when was the last time you washed these clothes?" Kairo held her nose together as she helped Cali with her bags. Kairo was on the verge of regurgitating from the foul stench of mildew.

"Oh girl, they been in the trunk forever in a day. These are my just in case clothes," Cali defended herself as they finally made it to Kairo's door. They stopped to catch their breath from lugging those foul, heavy clothes.

"So, where you trying to go tonight?" Kairo asked, because she already had plans to meet Delano tonight.

"Girl, some club called The Black Stallion. TJ and I saw the flyer on the counter. It's supposed to be a grand opening tonight," Cali responded, reaching into her back pocket handing Kairo a card that resembled the one Delano gave her earlier.

"Ok, it's a bet," Kairo said, as they walked into the condo, forgetting all about the talk they were supposed to have.

Kairo and Cali began getting ready for the club, listening to "Wax Tax n Dre Mix" while applying their makeup and drinking Carlo Rossi Moscato Sangria wine. That night Kairo wore a sleeveless red latex dress from Fashion Nova, along with some black Alexander McQueen platforms. Her body was sculpted just right with not a trace of fat on her stomach. Her ass was naturally round and plump with a set of perky double D's for breasts. Now Cali, on the other hand, was not as blessed in those areas as Kairo. Cali was part Caucasian and Black and she had no shape whatsoever. Kairo applied one more coat of red lipstick before they left out to the club.

FIFTEEN MINUTES LATER, they arrived at The Black Stallion and this club was indeed the top of the line. Delano had a red carpet laid out front and the grand opening lights beamed all over, shining through the night sky. The music was so loud you could hear "Ball" by T.I. ft. Lil' Wayne on the outside. The line was so long, it was stretching from Detroit to Africa.

Kairo could barely find a parking space, it was just that packed, so she ended up having to pay $20 for VIP parking. She didn't want to take a chance of getting her shit stolen. You know you can't have shit in Detroit.

"What's up bitches!!!?" TJ greeted them, wearing his bright neon pink suit exposing his chest. Matching with some pink neon open toe heels.

"Damn, my baby, you are looking bright tonight," Cali said, putting out her cancer stick. She always had to smoke a cigarette to cover up her real addiction, which no one knew about not even Kairo.

"Yes honey, while Kairo over here looking like a whole ass delicious candy apple," TJ complimented Kairo, poking his lips out, putting one hand on his hip and snapping his two fingers. Kairo did a little spin showing off her amazingly sculpted body before joining Cali in the line.

"Fuuuck, this line about long as hell," Cali complained as they stood in the line for entry.

"Don't worry, you know I got us." TJ flaunted his way between Cali and Kairo. "Wait for my signal and then y'all come up front."

TJ walked over to a tall, muscular man who was guarding the door. They exchanged a couple of words and just like that, TJ signaled for them to come up front. All you heard was people smacking lips and calling them all kinds of bitches and hoes because they stood in line for two hours.

"What the hell TJ, how you do that?" Kairo was curious how they just cut a whole ass two-hour line.

"Don't worry about all dat, just get ya ass in," TJ said, grabbing Kairo's hand, pulling her inside the club.

"Big Bank" by YG ft. 2 Chains, Nicki Minaj and Big Sean was now blasting through the speakers. The dancers were going crazy to this song, shaking their asses and twirling tricks on the silver, smooth, glittery pole while money was being tossed in the air.

"Now this what the fuck I'm talking about." Cali rushed through the crowd with TJ and Kairo in tow. "Free drinks until 12." Cali drowned her shot of 1800 and left for the dance floor.

Kairo really wasn't a big drinker, she just kept it simple, Grey Goose on the rocks. Now TJ, on the other hand, already ordered him three shots of Patrón and tossed them down back to back.

"So, are you gone tell me what you did to get us to get in front of the line?" Kairo asked, screaming in TJ's ear, trying to make conversation over the loud music.

"Oh, yea bitch." TJ started twerking on his seat. "You know ya boy got a throat for the dick," TJ said dramatically.

"Well I can only imagine how you sucked it," Kairo said, assuming he already did the deed, taking small sips of her Grey Goose.

"You mean how I'm gone suck it? This time I'm gone try something new. I'm gone use ice cream," TJ said, finally sitting down from all that dancing to the club music.

"ICE CREAM!" Kairo screamed, spitting the little drink she had out. She was shocked he would even do some shit like that. Now she was a pro at sucking dick, but never had she sucked one with ice cream. TJ chuckled, sipping on his strawberry Patrón reciting "1942" by G-Eazy, Yo Gotti, YNB Nahmir lyrics.

"Yes bitch, first you put the ice cream in your mouth and let it melt, do the hurricane on his dick making his ass bust in less than 10 motha-fucking minutes!" TJ said, too excited off his accomplishment he made up.

"Ok, what the fuck is the hurricane?" Kairo asked, curious because she just might have to add this to her playbook. TJ began talking, and Kairo started to drift away, slowly scanning the club for Delano. She saw no signs of him. *Why the fuck would he tell me to meet him here if he's not here?* she thought to herself. "Excuse me, I need to go to the ladies' room," Kairo said, leaving TJ at the bar and making her way through the full crowd.

She finally spotted Delano in group of men laughing and having a good ass time. The light shined directly on him, so she couldn't miss him. Kairo didn't know if it was her or the liquor, because he didn't look anything like he did earlier. In fact, he looked even more attractive than this morning. She guessed because he was in regular street clothes and not in his work clothes. His goatee was nicely trimmed, and he had a fresh line up around his 360 waves. Delano was wearing black jeans with a black Burberry button up and black Burberry loafers. He was smiling and rubbing his beard, flashing those perfect white teeth.

Kairo's pussy walls began to clutch together, just from watching him from across the room. She was imagining what it would be like if he was in between her thighs. The more and more she stared at him, the more and more her pussy got wet, creating a damn waterfall. Looking back, Kairo had the worse luck with men, she could never get a man that was there mentally. They would always say they would do one thing and their actions show another. She was tired of falling for these hood niggas, she wanted a man that was educated, street smart and of course attractive like Delano. As she was walking back to the bar, Kairo passed a group of drunk men and one of them decided to grab her arm.

"Well, aren't you pretty? How about we go in the back and do something strange for a piece of change?" the drunk man said, holding onto her wrist tightly. He was looking like a homeless man wearing baggy clothes that didn't even fit him.

"No thank you, but can you let me go?" she asked politely, trying to break free from his tight grip.

"Nah. Nah what's stopping me from taking yo' pretty ass back there right now and getting what I want?" he said, leaning in closer towards her. She turned her face away because she could smell the liquor on his foul breath.

"Please, can you let me go?" Kairo begged and pleaded, but this man was not trying to let her go. Now Kairo could have knocked this man straight off his feet, but she wasn't about to ruin the grand opening, although she had every right to protect herself.

"Is there a problem here?" Delano asked, stepping between the drunk man and Kairo. "She said let her go!" Delano forced the drunk hand to let go of her wrist. The drunk man waved his hand in Delano's face.

"Nah boss, no problems, I was just telling miss pretty how beautiful she is," the drunken man replied, sounding like he wanted no problems.

"Good, 'cause if you touch her again, I'm gon' break yo' fucking hand." Delano turned to walk away from the man, but the drunk man wasn't done talking. He ran up in Delano's face trying to prove a point.

"Nigga, I just said I didn't want no problems HERE!!" He was now jumping in Delano's face spitting and yelling. Next thing you know, Delano launched off and punched the drunk man in the mouth.

"OOOH SHIIIT!!!" the crowd hooted as they just witnessed Delano punching the helpless man in the mouth, busting his bottom lip. He straightened his button up, walking away as if he didn't just punch a man into a coma. The drunk man's entourage began causing a ruckus in the club, so Delano called a group of security men to escort them out.

2

KING OF THE SOUTH

G oddamn, *that shit hurt,* Delano thought to himself as he shook the hand he just used to punch this man into a coma, and didn't feel bad about it. Delano's knuckles began to bleed immediately. The impact from the blow must have been hard. It was always afterward when you start to feel the effects. This was the first night of his grand opening and he was already knocking niggas to sleep. He wasn't about to let any nigga touch Kairo, or any man touch the women in here. This was his establishment. He wished a nigga would come up to the club trying to regulate his shit. Delano picked up his cup of Hennessey and Kairo noticed his bloody knuckles.

"Oh my goodness Delano, you're bleeding," Kairo said, getting up to attend to Delano's hand. He was being stubborn, thinking it would make him less of a man if he responded to his bloody knuckles. So, she rushed over to the bar to get some ice to reduce the swelling.

"Thank you, I really appreciate your help," Delano said, watching as Kairo attended his hand, wrapping the bandages around, carefully applying pressure to stop the bleeding.

Delano smiled at Kairo, admiring the way she cared for him. She was his childhood crush, and he still felt strongly about her ever since they were kids. Maybe if life never got in the way, she would be his wife and the mother of his kids, but life sometimes took a detour. When his mother passed, he had to move down south with his father. Separated from Kairo for over 10 years, he spent every moment memorizing everything about her from her birthdate down to her favorite food to eat.

As he got older, Delano searched all over for her. He even went as far as hiring a private investigator, but still had no luck. Even if Kairo was to remember who Delano was, she wouldn't be able to recognize him right off because he grew into his looks. Delano didn't always have facial hair or muscles, he just used to be tall and skinny. He was determined to get her attention so he waited for an opportunity to get her alone so he could strike up a conversation while sitting at the bar.

"So, what are you drinking tonight?" Delano asked, volunteering to buy her a drink.

"Oh, I'm not really drinking anything but Grey Goose," Kairo replied, taking a sip from the cylinder glass and shifting in her chair showing off her thick thighs. She had always been a beautiful woman. Mixed with Black and Native American, her skin was soft as butter, brown like mahogany.

"You sure? You know you can order anything you want tonight, drinks on the house," Delano asked her again.

"Oh, ok, well that's nice to know, but I'm gone stick to my Grey Goose." Kairo flagged the bartender down. "Can I get another Grey Goose smooth on the rocks?"

"Do you mind if we go somewhere and talk?" Delano asked, extending his hand helping her out her seat, taking her to a booth by VIP. When Delano last saw Kairo, she was skinny with a squeaky voice, and now she was more beautiful than ever. He loved how her body filled that little red dress and how good she smelled. As he began to visualize what her pussy tasted like, his dick began to jump in his pants.

"This is really nice. The club is banging from wall to wall," Kairo complimented, sipping from her glass, admiring the color lighting that was flashing around the club. Delano really invested a lot of his money into this club. He was hoping to turn away from the drug life and operate a legal business right here in Downtown Detroit. He was halfway there, he just needed to step away from the fast money.

"Yes, thank you, my team and I worked our asses off to get this club started," Delano said, hoping it would impress her. He really wasn't about impressing any female, but Kairo, she was different.

"Word, this your establishment?" She batted her eyes, placing her hand over her heart.

"Yes ma'am, all this is mine, from the dancers to the DJ. I own all of this." Delano smiled, looking around trying to pretend like he wasn't flattered by her reaction. He guessed his impression did work after all. He took a sip of his Hennessey and sat back admiring the beauty that was in front of him. Tonight was the best night of his life, that was until he had to tell her the truth.

"If you keep knocking folks into a damn coma, you not gone have no business," Kairo advised, adjusting in her seat, applying another coat of red lipstick.

"I know, but I had to protect you," Delano admitted, remembering his promise he made to God. That if Kairo and he ever crossed paths again, he would protect her with all his life.

"Protect me from what?" Kairo asked, now twisting her face up. She was confused and didn't understand why Delano wasn't being clear with her. She was the easiest person to talk to, but Delano had to make it difficult.

Soon as Delano could open his mouth to speak, his publicist walked up snatching him out of Kairo's presence. He had to be ready in less than three minutes to give his grand opening speech. He approached the stage and the crowd began to roar, Lano! Lano! He glanced back over his shoulders to see if Kairo was still sitting in the spot he left her. To his surprise, she was no longer sitting there. *Where the fuck did she go so quickly?* Delano thought to himself. He had to find her, or else she would be in great danger.

He couldn't leave the stage fast enough to set out searching for Kairo. She didn't return to the booth where he left her. He then thought maybe she went to the ladies' room, but she wasn't there either. He asked his staff if they saw her, but no one was able to recognize the woman he described. He searched all over, except the bar. Walking through the crowd, he finally spotted a very tipsy Kairo sitting there with her friends.

"Kairo, I thought I told you to wait for me," Delano said in a calm voice, approaching her as she sipped her drink. TJ, checking Delano out, looked him up and down taking a seat next to Kairo, crossing his legs.

"Well aren't you rude?" TJ said, griming at him. He didn't like Delano trying to steal his only company, because Cali was out on the dance floor dancing.

"TJ, behave yourself," Kairo said, cutting him the nasty eye before talking to Delano. "My bad, I didn't want to leave my friends. This is TJ," she introduced the two. Then Cali finally came back from the dance floor, not expecting to see Delano.

"Wow, Delano Harris? What are the odds of seeing you here tonight?" a very drunk Cali said trying to hug him. He gave Cali a fake smile, just to keep the atmosphere sane. Delano and Cali had a past, and things didn't end too well because of his obsession with Kairo. Cali turned her back to get a shot of 1800, and that's when he noticed a familiar tattoo on her right upper shoulder.

"I'm sorry, do y'all know each other?" Kairo asked, unaware of their past. Cali didn't hear what she asked, so Delano shook his head no quickly, lying. In fact, he knew Cali very well, he just didn't want to talk about how.

"Kairo, can you come here please?" Delano asked, leading her over to a secluded area to get away from the crowd. Kairo put her hands around her curvy hips, trying to understand what was going on. She was buzzing from the liquor and could barely stand straight. "You had me worried. I was looking for you all over." Delano was looking into Kairo's eyes, holding onto her shoulders.

Kairo nervously chuckled. She wasn't used to any man looking for her. She was always used to getting looked over.

"What? I'm grown as hell, why are you acting so damn paranoid? You've literally been on tip since earlier," she snapped, pushing her straight hair in the back and crossing her arms.

"Kairo, look at me. Do you even remember who I am?" Delano asked nervously. He already had a feeling she didn't remember him. She paused to look at him, and then shook her head no. "You don't remember me?" he asked again.

"No motherfucka, you are acting sketchy! Don't nobody have time for this cat and mouse game you're trying to play," she fumed, walking away. Delano had to think quickly, Kairo was slipping out of his hands like butter.

"It was the summer of 2003, when we first met at the Boys and Girls Club off Collingwood!" Delano shouted so loud that Kairo stopped. She doubled back towards him, looking at him, squinting her eyes to try to familiarize his face. "You won't recognize me. We were kids then and I look nothing like how I used to because now I have facial hair," Delano said as she was still processing his face.

"Earlier you said you knew me, so how do you know me?" Kairo asked. Delano led Kairo back over to the same secluded area where they were originally sitting.

"Ok, you know after lunch time we would play four square outdoors followed by dodge ball in the gym?" Kairo nodded in agreement, and Delano continued. "You were so terrified the ball was going to hit your skinny ass, you never played. You and a couple of girls would go behind the green curtain and have singing competitions with the other girls. I thought you had the most angelic voice." Delano was passionate as he spoke.

"Wow, I was young as hell. How do you still remember that?" She leaned in closer, he now had her full attention.

"Believe it or not, I paid a lot of attention to you. I also remember when you fell and scraped your knee climbing the fence." Delano was hoping it would help jog her memory, because he also climbed that same fence.

Kairo grabbed her face. "Oh shit, your name was Delani then. Why did you change your name?" she questioned, because she had simply forgotten about him. She vaguely remembered if they had a conversation together, just knew they spoke in passing.

"Yes, that name was too girlie for me. My father changed it."

Delano took a sip of his drink and sat back into the booth putting his arms around Kairo.

"Ok, now I remember. You were always in the office because you kept getting into trouble. I wondered what happened to you." She started to remember slowly, little by little. Then it clicked in her mind that this was how come he knew her so well.

"Yea, my moms passed, and I moved down south with my father," Delano said, taking another sip.

"Oh, I'm sorry to hear that!" Kairo said with her hand over her heart. She knew what it was like to lose someone close. She'd lost all four of her older brothers.

"It's alright. I also had the biggest crush on you when we were kids," Delano finally admitted. He couldn't get that out right away. It was something about Kairo that made him freeze up every time. Delano knew he was attractive, but it was how Kairo carried herself like she wasn't for any bullshit.

"What!" Kairo screamed, covering her mouth. "Shut the fuck up, no you didn't. Why'd you never say anything?" she asked, looking at Delano with awe.

"I never said anything because I'm three years older than you. I felt it was wrong, since at the time you were 11. Girl, you don't know all the trouble I've been through trying to find you," Delano said, pulling her closer to him so their bodies were touching. "I don't ever want to lose you again."

"Well, long as you don't fuck up, you won't lose me." A super tipsy Kairo leaned in closer to kiss him, but Delano pulled away for two reasons. One, he knew when he told Kairo the truth, he would lose her forever and two, he was already romantically involved with someone else. "What's wrong?" she asked, placing her hand on his back, stroking it as he sat there contemplating if he was going to tell the truth.

"Kairo, you want to know the truth? I was hired to torture and kill you," Delano spoke bluntly, finally getting it off his chest. It wasn't in his intentions to kill her either. Johnny hired him to do a hit that he agreed to do, and he didn't know it was Kairo until Johnny showed him a picture of her.

"What? You were hired to to-to-torture and ki-ki-ll me?" she asked, choking on her words.

"Yes, the truck you drive, Johnny owns it. You been behind on your payments for quite some time now. He ordered the hit a month ago," Delano said, refilling his glass with Hennessey.

"Wait, so you are a hit man? Why didn't you do it?" She was feeling uneasy about everything. Kairo's heart was beating furiously. She knew she was fucked up but to go as far as killing her, now this Johnny was reaching.

"Nah, I'm more than just a hit man baby. Besides, I didn't know it was you until he showed me your picture. Since I found out, I spent countless nights wondering how I was going to avoid having to hurt you," Delano revealed. He was now getting frustrated, thinking about all the trouble this was going to cause between him and Johnny. He wasn't sure how he was going to avoid Johnny killing her. He had the whole city working as informants.

"Well that explains why you're so damn paranoid. Your heart and feelings got in the way," Kairo mentioned, crossing her legs across each other. "You didn't do any better bringing me to the damn slaughterhouse either."

Delano had to pause and think. She was right, but he had his reasons. He wanted to protect her if he could. So, he did what he thought was necessary. He got her where he wanted her.

"I know, it was the only way I knew you were in my protection. Trust me, Johnny is already hip about you. He has the whole east side working for him," Delano said, contemplating about what to do next.

"You told me you paid the note earlier, did you not do it?" she huffed, twisting her head to the side.

"Yes, I been paid it a while ago actually, but it didn't stop the hit. So, I rented a uniform and a truck from some dude named Tyrone so I could find a way to contact you," Delano admitted to her.

"That was very clever of you. I thank you for not killing me," Kairo said, expressing her gratitude that Delano spared her life. He nodded and took a sip of the rest of his Hennessey while Cali and TJ approached their booth.

"Well, it's getting late. TJ and I are about to head out of here," Cali said, leaving with TJ. She waved goodbye at Delano, but he just looked away and Kairo caught that. Even though Kairo was tipsy, she still was able to see the animosity between the two, she just couldn't figure out what it was. She wasn't about to figure out either, maybe if she had, she would be able to avoid what was to come.

"Oh, this is my song!!" Kairo said as she moved her body slowly to "Come Through and Chill" by Miguel ft. J. Cole and Salaam Remi. It was two am and the music started to slow down as the club was closing. The staff was left cleaning up as Kairo and Delano helped themselves to some more drinks. They were having such a good time catching up, they didn't realize the time flew by and it was now three am.

"How about I change the music, you know, lighten up the mood a bit," Delano said as he was shuffling through his music playlist that was connected to the club speakers. He chose "Between the Sheets" by The Isley Brothers and began to strip tease in front of Kairo, taking his clothes off little by little. "I hope I'm not scaring you," Delano said, pulling Kairo out of her seat onto the white, tempered glass stage.

"No, I'm not scared. I'm from Dexter, so I was raised with a gun in my hand," Kairo stated, gulping the rest of her drink down.

"Damn, slow down. That's hard liquor you're drinking!" he warned her, because she was straight knocking her drink back. Kairo didn't give a damn about that. The only thing she had on her mind was some of Delano's penis inside her.

"I'll be fine. You only live once, right?" she asked, pushing Delano onto the white stage. Now straddling herself on top of him, she was making it hard for him to concentrate. His dick was hard as hell just from the warmth that flowed between her thighs.

"Damn girl, can you warn a nigga first? You got my dick about hard as a rock," Delano said as he was trading places with Kairo. She was now sitting up, looking Delano directly in his eyes.

"Well, life's too short to waste on just talking," she whispered seductively in his ear, pulling Delano close as she began to unbutton his shirt. Running her fingers back and forth, circling around his tribal tattoo, he didn't know what he was getting himself into, but he was down for whatever.

"Shit girl, you gone get me in troub—" Delano said, but was interrupted by Kairo.

"Shhh! Less talking, more of me." A very seductive Kairo placed her finger on Delano's lips silencing him. Delano so badly wanted to tear that ass up, but he had a woman at home with their son. He never stepped out on his woman before, but Kairo was different. He didn't exactly stop her either. Delano continued to allow Kairo to seduce him because he was intrigued by her. He felt like, what Nikki don't know won't hurt her. Kairo proceeded to unzip his pants, pulling out his eight inches into her watery mouth. *Slurp, Slurp, Slurp,* she made the slurping sounds, twirling her tongue around the head.

"Fuck girl, you so nasty! Come give daddy a kiss," Delano said as he licked his pink lips. She did exactly as he said to do. Continuing to deep throat him, she made gagging noises, tightening her lips around his shaft. The way she slowly sucked his dick made him groan. Delano never got head so good like this before.

"Mmmm, daddy!" Kairo moaned, looking up at Delano as he continued guiding her head back and forth.

Kairo got up and laid back on her back before he removed her thongs, planting sloppy kisses on the inside of her thick, juicy thighs. He enjoyed inhaling the sweet smell of her vagina that was glistening and leaking like a waterfall. Kairo gently moaned as he kissed around her perfectly shaved pussy.

Damn her pussy fat. I can't wait to taste it, Delano thought to himself as he slowly licked the clitoris down to her anus. Using his big tongue like a mop, he began to eat her pussy like it was a clean-up on aisle four in pussyland.

"Oh shit, I'm about to squirt!!!!" Kairo screamed as she reached an orgasm. Her body began to tremble and shake uncontrollably before spewing water everywhere like a water faucet. "Fuck me!!!!" she yelled, holding Delano's head in place, causing his tongue to slide in

Delano was in the fridge pouring himself a glass of milk to calm his high. She began swinging the bat in the air as if she was going to hit him. She knew better than to hit Delano; she was too scary.

"Nikki you know where the fuck I've been," Delano said, irritated, walking away from her. "And put that damn bat down, you're acting crazy."

"It's five in the morning Delano! Johnny said your club should have closed at two, explain that!" Nikki was screaming and pointing her long nails in Delano's face. He felt like she could have come out to support him. After all, they were together.

Females always want the title but never the responsibility that comes along with it, Delano thought to himself, almost saying it out loud. He didn't feel like arguing. He already knew how Nikki was, always had to be the one that had the last word.

So, he began tuning Nikki's nagging ass out and started thinking about Kairo. His dick grew hard in his pants, reminiscing on tonight's events with her. He got aroused thinking about how good Kairo's pussy tasted.

"Shut up and come here," Delano said, sloppily kissing Nikki, imagining it was Kairo's soft lips. He held Nikki close picking her up on the counter, still kissing her.

"Whh-what are you doing?" Nikki stammered as she kissed Delano back.

"Hush, you gone ruin it," Delano hissed, still kissing her and then taking her to their bed. Imagining she was Kairo, he devoured her pussy like it was his favorite fruit. He never really ate Nikki's pussy like that, especially like he was now.

"Goddamn, you never ate my pussy like thiiiis!" Nikki moaned out loud grabbing Delano's head. She was about to damn near tear his head off. S,he screamed locking her legs around his neck.

He continued to eat her pussy, gently squeezing her breast playing with her nipples. Making a trail of licks up to her neck and finally putting all eight inches inside of Nikki, he was still pretending she was Kairo. He made slow and steady thrusts, imagining how she felt. He spread Nikki's ass cheeks closer to his body and thrusted deeper into her pussy. Imagination could be a motherfucka. He was no longer in love with her, so their sex life was no longer a thrill. He quickened his pace as he was coming close to nutting, and he thought of Kairo's tight lips wrapped around his pole.

"AHHHHHH!!!" Delano groaned as he exploded inside Nikki. He was thankful she was on birth control, because he was not trying to have another baby with her. He was no longer in love with her, simply because he was in love with somebody else. Plus, Nikki had become this nagging, controlling, manipulative bitch within the last two years.

Delano had no desire to rule the streets, but Nikki wanted him to stay the way he was because the money was fast. He never asked to be a king pin, it was just given to him once his father died. He was more into building houses from scratch, flipping them and selling them on the market. Nikki reminded him of the man he no longer wanted to be.

"Goddamn, you ain't never fucked me like that! What made you fuck me like that?" she asked, getting up to wipe herself off. Delano wasn't in the mood for pillow talking, so he just rolled over and went to sleep without saying another word.

THE NEXT MORNING, while Nikki was still sleep, Delano took a hot shower and slid on his grey Nike fit with his wheat Timbs. He was excited to see Kairo and couldn't wait to see her. Since she was without a phone to call him, he cashed her out a brand-new iPhone 11. He wanted to provide for her, and he was determined to show her. *She would really like this,* Delano said to himself as he made his way down Kairo's block. Finally reaching her condo, he knocked and knocked but got no answer. *What if Johnny got her before I could get her out?* Delano thought to himself as he was turning around to go back to his truck. One of her neighbors peeked their heads out their door catching Delano just in time.

"You are looking for Kairo?" one of her neighbors asked.

"Yes, have you seen her?" Delano was walking back towards to them.

"The police came and got her earlier, she's at the police station," they said and slammed the door in his face before Delano could even ask which station. Delano quickly speed-dialed Jimenez, his in-house attorney.

"What's up boss?" Jimenez answered within the first ring.

"Jimenez, I need you to be Kairo's attorney. I think something bad has happened," Delano spoke into the phone. He wasn't sure what was going on, but it would be smart if he sent Jimenez and not himself. Delano and cops didn't get along well, just like any other drug dealer in town.

"Damn blood, who is Kairo? Do you know which precinct she's at?" Jimenez asked, because he'd never met her before. This was his first time hearing of another woman's name from Delano's mouth.

"She is just a friend of mine. I recently just ran into her yesterday. Plus, she is good people and I'm assuming since I'm East, the ninth precinct, which is the one on Gunston and Gratiot," Delano provided Jimenez with all the information he needed.

"Alright, say less. I'm in route right now." Jimenez stopped doing whatever he was doing to help Delano out.

"That's what's up. Check your account, I just wired you $10,000 in cash. Call me as soon you leave with her at the station," he commanded.

"Alright," Jimenez said as he disconnected the call.

Delano jumped into his truck tossing the phone into the passenger seat and headed straight over to Johnny's house. He needed to get out this game. At one point in time, Johnny and Delano were cool. Johnny used to buy his product though Delano and the Colombians. That's until Johnny switched up and joined the Italians as his new connect instead. Knowing the Italians were sworn enemies to Delano and the Colombians.

When Johnny heard Delano was expanding his territory up north, he hurried up and sealed a deal with his father. He suggested Delano serve Johnny to keep the peace between the north and south cartels. Which at the time, Delano's father was his trusted advisor before he passed away. Soon as Delano landed in Detroit two years ago, Johnny had him working as his personal hit man instead of giving him the drug trade on the westside of Detroit. That was the original deal he made with his father, but Johnny forfeited the deal first. Now it was time for Johnny to pay the fuck up.

Delano pulled up to Johnny's mansion off Jefferson and parked his big truck right on the grass. Fuck having respect, because he had none for Johnny. Two big men dressed in black rushed towards him with guns in their hands. Delano was a fearless man, so they didn't intimidate him. He reached for his Glock 87 from his waist and pulled it out on them.

"Let him through!" Johnny yelled from the table where he was eating breakfast. The two men fell back allowing Delano to pass them. "So, to what do I owe this pleasure?" Johnny asked, stuffing his mouth with scrambled eggs.

"I want out, out this fucked up triangle you are running," Delano said angrily, trying to hide the true reason why he wanted out.

Johnny took a sip of his orange juice that was in a champagne glass and busted out laughing. He thought Delano was joking with him. Delano took his Glock 87 and aimed it at one of his guards, shooting him directly between his eyes right on the nose bridge. This caused Johnny to stop laughing, choking on his spit, and his eyes widened. He couldn't believe Delano just came into his house shooting his men.

"Nigga, does it look like I'm laughing with you?" Delano asked, stepping closer to Johnny.

"You can't come in my house demanding shit and killing my men. We had a deal, you kill Kairo. You did not, instead, you let the bitch live." Johnny was clenching his jaws, displaying his anger, and rushed over to the man that was just shot.

"We did have a deal. You broke that when you never gave me the westside. Then you asked me to kill someone I'm close too. Hell no, I'm not working for you anymore!!" Delano was furious and forgot about keeping his shit in check.

Johnny looked up from checking his guard's pulse and said, "Nigga, don't tell me you'd rather lose your life over some bitch."

Johnny's words kindled Delano's anger even more. He looked at Johnny directly in the eyes and pointed the gun in his face.

"You can't kill me, but I can kill you." Delano wasn't hesitating to pull the trigger, but he spared his life anyway. Just as Johnny was the most powerful man in Detroit, well, Delano held just as much clout in New Orleans, Louisiana.

"If you want out, then the south and north will be back at war," Johnny said, confirming he was going back on his word about the two cartels not going to war. Johnny never kept his word. He felt like since Delano's father was dead, the deal no longer stood.

"War it is then." Delano shook his head and walked away. He couldn't believe Johnny, but he should have known better. Johnny was blood thirsty. After all, it was Delano that introduced him to this drug lifestyle when they were younger. He knew Johnny could take over Detroit's drug cartel by his careless demeanor, and that's what exactly Johnny did. No matter who he had to kill to get where he was now.

3

SMILING FACES

The time was nine o'clock on a Saturday morning, when Cali woke up to indistinct chatter over her head as she sat down at the ninth precinct. There Cali and Kairo sat in separate holding rooms, as they waited patiently for the detectives to come question them about Mr. Banks' murder.

Like one of the legendary groups from Motown, "The Undisputed Truth," once said, *smiling faces tell lies and don't tell the truth*. Well, that's what Cali had, a *"Smiling Face."* She was one sneaky, conniving female and could not be trusted.

She couldn't help it, betrayal and deceit were her parents and it was all she knew. The truth didn't live in Cali, everything was a lie that rolled off her tongue. Her nickname should be two-tongued snake, because her ways were poison. Then she turned around and played the victim like how she was playing the game with the police. After all, she was Johnny's oldest sister, so she was untouchable, protected by the notorious Detroit kingpin. Cali had to be sitting in that interrogation room for one or two hours. It felt like four hours before the detective investigating the case finally entered the room.

"Miss Jones, thank you for waiting. I'm Detective Kaz and this is my partner Sergeant Hooper. We're investigating the murder of Peter

Banks which occurred this morning between the times of two and six am," the detective said, handing Cali a small cup of hot coffee. Cali took a deep breath and nodded her head so they could proceed with the interrogation.

"Is this your former boss?" Detective Kaz predicted, showing her a photo of Mr. Banks.

"Yes, that's him. Kairo and I both used to worked for him." Cali was crying, putting on some fake tears, pretending like she was emotional. She had to make it look and sound believable that she was innocent. When it really was her who pulled the trigger, trying to pin the murder on Kairo.

"Ok, can you start from the beginning of what occurred yesterday?" Detective Kaz asked, adjusting the camera to record Cali's statement. Cali felt like she was on the *First 48* and zoned out. In a way she was nervous, because she didn't know what to expect of Delano. She knew she was wrong for trying to pin this murder on Kairo, but she had to get Kairo in the death chair.

Cali had her reasons why she deceived to be Kairo's friend, it all was part of an act. This was an act of revenge, because Cali truly believed Kairo was the cause to why she and Delano's relationship didn't last. Meanwhile, half of that was true. Cali was just something to do while Delano patiently waited for Kairo to become of age.

They were young and Cali wasn't expecting to fall in love with Delano, it just happened. He was the first relationship she was comfortable with opening up about her abusive past from her father Johnny Sr. He was abusive in all kinds of ways you could imagine. He was a big-time pimp in San Diego, California and New York City. Cali's mother was his lead prostitute, until he killed her for no reason, coldblooded in front of Cali when she was only three years old.

Taking Cali and fleeing to New York City, where he met Johnny Jr.'s mother, she also died from a drug overdose. With two small kids to feed, the prostitutes weren't bringing enough money in so he began pushing dope on the side. Money still was tight so he would sell his kids to strangers, allowing them to do anything sexual that they pleased.

By the time Cali was 14 and Johnny Jr was 11, they moved on Petoskey and Otsego in Detroit. That's when Cali and Delano first met, because they lived one house away from each other. Cali would run away to his house whenever their father had been abusive towards them. Their relationship became stagnant after they had sex and she got pregnant their first time. She never got the chance to tell Delano she was pregnant because they moved away. She was forced to give the baby up for adoption after their father was indicted on numerous counts, sending him to prison without parole. Cali and Johnny both were separated by the state, going from foster home to foster home.

"California Jones!!" Detective Kaz snapped her fingers in Cali's face, waking her out her trance. "Are you ok?"

"I'm sorry, what now?" Cali asked because she simply forgot what she supposed to be saying.

"I need you to give your statement on what happened yesterday on Friday, June 14th?"

Cali began telling a story, one lie after another, while the detectives were nodding their heads and writing her statement down. Although it wasn't true, they seemed to have bought her story. She made sure last night she stole Kairo's phone when Delano first pulled her away. She called Mr. Banks off Kairo's phone, pretending like she was stranded at the liquor store on Mack and Bewick, luring him into a death trap. They left and fucked behind South Eastern High School and 15 minutes later, she shot him in the head. She planted Kairo's phone in his car, so when the police arrived, they would have found it.

The detectives left the room to meet with Jimenez and to talk amongst one another. With the evidence all pointing towards Kairo, Cali was positive she was going down for this murder. She couldn't even remember half the shit she said, she just knew it sounded good. Cali was just talking because she had a mouth, and nothing ever good came out of it.

Thinking back, yesterday was Cali's first time seeing Delano in years. She never expected to see him again. After being forced to give their son Malachi up for adoption, she spent every moment trying to reconcile their relationship. It was too late, his heart belonged to someone else. That someone else was Kairo. Cali spent years stalking Kairo, before joining the same college as her. Since then, Cali was smiling in Kairo's face but really staying close just to watch her fall. Shortly, the detectives returned into the room.

"Thank you for your time Miss Jones, however, we are unable to obtain enough evidence to keep you in custody. You are being released," Detective Kaz said as they dismissed her. Cali walked out and was smiling from ear to ear. She felt like she accomplished letting Kairo take the fall. Little did she know, her little plan was going to backfire. Cali might have been conniving, but she wasn't clever at all. The detectives knew she was lying, because Jimenez brought a surveillance tape placing Kairo at the club with Delano between the hours of 10 pm and 5 am. The video was like a porn to them, but they saw what they needed to see and that Kairo was innocent. They could have charged her with false reporting, but they knew she was Johnny's sister and didn't want any trouble with him.

As Cali was leaving out, Kairo was standing next to some Hispanic man who appeared to be a lawyer posting her bail. She was dressed in her pink house coat still, with her bonnet on her head. The police didn't give her time to change they just brought her to the station. Kairo looked up and saw Cali walking past in the hallway. So, she decided to go speak, still unaware that it was Cali who set her up.

"Yo, Cali, wait up. Did you know Mr. Banks was killed last night?" Kairo said as she approached Cali, playfully hitting her in the left arm. Cali jumped like she'd seen a ghost, she really felt guilty for what she had done. Kairo peeped how nervous she was. "Bitch, what is wrong with you? Why you acting so nervous?" Kairo asked.

"Nothing, I'm just sad he died. Now how am I going to pay my rent?" Cali lied. She had to think of something quick or Kairo would have caught on. Cali zipped up her pink and grey North Face jacket, taking a seat in the lobby. Kairo sat down next to her, she thought Cali was hiding something. She just didn't know what it was yet.

"Cali, if you know anything, please tell the police," Kairo said, getting up to walk with Jimenez out the police station. Cali began to think what if shit didn't go according to plan? She never framed anyone before. She couldn't even step outside fast enough, before she was approached by two muscular men dressed in black.

"You need to come with us," they said as they instructed Cali to get inside Johnny's black Escalade.

"Damn, took you long enough to get me out!" Cali complained because it took him more than an hour to pick her up when he was no more than 15 minutes away. Johnny just sat there and blew a cloud of smoke in Cali's face from his strawberry-flavored hookah. For Johnny to be a ruthless leader, he was one tall, handsome, dark-skinned man with dreads.

"Can I get at least a hello brother, how about how are you? You just get in my truck and start bitching," Johnny scolded as he straightened his white tee. He had two heavy 14k chains draped around his neck.

"Bitching? You sound just like our father. He was forever quick to call me a bitch," Cali responded with an attitude, unaware of what was about to happened next. Johnny slapped the fuck out of her. He slapped Cali so hard her nose began to bleed. Tears were now forming in the corner of Cali's eyes as she sat there holding her left cheek.

"Don't you ever compare me to that nigga. I'm nothing like him. If anything, I'm better!" Johnny yelled, pointing his boney finger in Cali's face. "You ever do that shit again, I'm gone decapitate your ass. Now get the fuck out my truck," Johnny threatened, giving Cali some cocaine. Cali hurried up and got out his truck. She hated how Johnny treated her like shit that came out his ass that you just flush down the toilet. You would think she wasn't his oldest blood sister by the way he treated her. Johnny had power, so he wasn't thinking about how anyone felt. He just wanted money, drugs and power.

Walking into the house, Don, the father of Cali's three smallest children, was already sitting in the living room. Cali took the bag of cocaine, spread it out on the table and started doing lines. No one knew Cali was a drug addict, not even Kairo or Delano. Only Johnny knew because he was her relative and dealer. Cali's drug addiction was the main reason she didn't have her children today.

In total, Cali had four children. Malachi was now 14, who she had with Delano but was forcefully given up for adoption. The other three, Avalon, five, Tyrik, four, and Arizona, two, were placed into the system. Cali could have been the perfect model for "fuck them kids," because she didn't give a fuck about those kids. All she cared about was love, money and cocaine.

That's how come she never got clean or went to go look for any of them. She figured they would be better off where they were. Cali didn't exactly have the best childhood either. She lost her mother at a young age and was sexually molested by her own father. Drugs were the only way she could find relief from her childhood scars.

"Damn, what happened to your face?" Don asked Cali as he sniffed a line, squeezing his nostrils together from the burning sensation. Cali ignored him and continued to snort two more lines back to back. Her body began to tingle as the drugs got her horny and aroused thinking about Delano.

"Fuck me!" Cali yelled at Don, aggressively taking his clothes off exposing his hard, chocolate dick. She got on her knees preparing to suck Don's dick, tying her hair up in a ponytail. She wanted to suck his dick real sloppy and nasty.

"Damn, you are a naughty bitch!" Don said, holding Cali's head in place so she could gag on his enormous dick that was now in the back of her throat. He stood up off the couch to throat fuck her, allowing Cali to gag and slob everywhere without using her hands.

"Fuck baby, suck this dick!" Don groaned as Cali began sucking his dick, licking his balls and eventually rimming him. She inserted a finger in his ass and stroked his dick at the same time. Don loved when Cali increased the speed of her fingers inside his ass and jerked him off to send his orgasm through the roof.

"Come swallow this nut, I'm about to bust." Don held Cali's face close as he nutted all on her face.

Cali slid her panties to the side and let Don enter inside her wet pussy from the back. POW! Don smacked her ass as he shoved his dick in and out.

"Put it in my ass!" Cali begged Don since it was something new they were trying.

"Not yet baby, let me tie you up." Don grabbed some straps and tied her down to the bed in their room.

Don began to lick Cali's pussy, slowly increasing the speed of his tongue on her clit, making her body shake into convulsions as she came all in his mouth. He then stuck all of his seven inches inside Cali's ass. She moaned in pain because he was inside her so deep and biting her earlobe. She wasn't used to anal sex, they only just started. He was pounding her ass like it was some pussy, groaning while his sweat was dripping down Cali's back.

"Don, switch up!" Cali whined, feeling the burning sensation from her anus. She was sure she was going to shit on herself if he didn't stop. He just kept going since he was so close to finishing.

"Hold on, I'm almost finished. I'm about cum." Don released himself inside Cali's ass and collapsed on top of her. He was panting so loud like a dog and out of breath, asking Cali to do something he never asked her to do before. He wanted her to push the cum back out as he licked it out her ass. Cali was so fucking high off the cocaine she wasn't even suspicious of her own damn man.

It was storming outside the next day when Cali awoke to the loud sound of thunder. The rain fell hard against the windowpane as she got up to close the window. *Bzzzz bzzzzz!* Cali's phone kept vibrating back to back. She ran to grab her phone off the nightstand before it woke up Don. There were multiple missed calls from Kairo and Johnny. Cali was avoiding Kairo, so she called Johnny back instead. He was calling an emergency meeting. Cali woke Don up so they could get dressed and headed straight over to the warehouse on Vandyke and Lynch. When they got there Johnny was standing in the middle of the warehouse with two Rottweilers, one on each side of him.

"Good morning, ladies and gentlemen, I called you here for two reasons. One, we are now going to war with the south and two, someone has the balls to steal from me!" Johnny said, clenching his jaws with anger in voice.

Cali had no clue who the fuck had the balls to steal from him, but they were going to wish they never did. She scanned the room to see if anybody was looking suspicious and each man and woman stood at attention like soldiers.

"Before we go to war, here is an opportunity to come forward and I will let you live," Johnny said, pointing the gun in each man's face. He was so furious his jaw kept clenching, and the next thing Cali heard was a gunshot. POOOW! Blood and brains splattered everywhere, some even got on her. Wails and cries came from the people in the warehouse who screamed because he killed Bubba, who was only 16 and wasn't the one who stole from him.

"I will start killing innocent people until someone comes forward. Release the Rottweilers!" Johnny said, wiping the blood off the gun, continuing to point it at them. People were terrified, afraid to breathe because the slightest movement could mean a bullet or eaten alive. They cried silently as they watched the dogs eat Bubba's body, tearing it apart limb from limb. Their teeth were gnashing at his skin, crunching down on his bones. This was something serious. Johnny had never killed someone in front of his own before, and he would normally torture them and make them disappear. Johnny fired another gunshot and another body fell to the ground, this time it was a woman.

"Come on Johnny, this is fucking insane," Cali wined, hoping it would stop this madness, but he just stood in front of her looking her in the eyes and walked away. Twenty minutes and five bodies later, someone by the name of Cameron came forward, placing the blame on Delano for stealing. It was easy to blame someone who was not there to defend themselves. He was unaware Delano was no longer working with them. Johnny knew automatically it was him, he was snitching on someone. In Detroit, snitching was a death sentence in the streets.

"Cameron, you were once Delano's partner before working alongside him making moves. It should occur to you that he is now the enemy. I'm going to give you two choices, get eaten alive or take a bullet, your choice," Johnny said, twirling the gun in his hand making the decision for him. Cameron chose to take the bullet, but Johnny set the dogs on him instead. The warehouse was filled with Cameron's screams echoing through the walls as he was getting ate alive. *POW POW POW!* The front of Johnny's gun barrel was smoking as he emptied the rest of his clip into Cameron's dead carcass.

"LET THIS BE A FUCKING LESSON!!! DON'T EVER FUCKING STEAL FROM ME! CLEAN THIS FUCKING SHIT UP!" Johnny shouted at everyone as they continued to mourn. That day, he killed seven people in cold blood. The warehouse was filled with a lot of commotion. Some lost friends, some lost family. Things would never be the same for Johnny. He was losing respect from some of his most loyal men.

"Well wasn't that some—" Cali said, looking behind her realizing Don was no longer there. *Where the fuck did he just disappear to? He was just standing behind me. Maybe he went to the men's room,* she assumed. Cali began fixing herself a plate of breakfast before searching the whole common area in the warehouse for Don.

Thirty minutes passed and there was still no sign of Don. Cali was ready to go, she had shit to do. So, she went to go use the bathroom before she caught an Uber home. When she got to the bathroom, she felt like a damn blow torch was being held close to her vagina lips. "Ahh," she yelped in pain as she wiped with the tissue and noticed blood. It couldn't be her monthly because she'd already had one. *What the fuck is going on?* she wondered, using her phone to google the symptoms trying to self-diagnose.

Cali had either of the three conditions—genital herpes, syphilis, or a urinary tract infection. She knew a urinary tract infection wasn't going to leave her with blisters. So, it had to be one of the other two. Deep down inside, she was praying to God it was neither. Cali washed her hands and then proceeded to leave out the restroom.

The sounds of light moans caught her attention. She decided to be nosy and walk down the hall to see if it was Don fucking another woman. Since he wanted to disappear out of nowhere, Cali knew she wasn't tripping. As she got closer, she heard someone screaming Don's name. Before Cali knew it, she was in front of Johnny's office. *What the fuck is going on in there?* she questioned herself, putting her right ear up to the door. She heard Don's familiar grunting and decided to open the door. The palms of her hands grew sweaty as she slowly turned the knob.

WHAT THE FUCK?!!!!!! Don had Johnny bent over, ramming his dick inside Johnny's ass. Cali stood there for five minutes paralyzed watching them fuck. She couldn't move. Her heart froze watching Don, the father of her three children, fucking her blood brother. They were too busy fucking to even notice Cali standing there. Don's dick was so hard you could see the veins pulsating as it went in and out of Johnny's creamy asshole finishing up. Don got on his knees licking his own cream pie out of Johnny's ass. This made Cali sick, because Don just did the same shit to her last night.

"So, this is what the fuck we are doing right now?" Cali said in a raging voice. She had every right to be emotional. The man she spent three years with was DL. Johnny hurried and pulled up his pants while Don was stuck like a deer caught in the headlights.

"Man, get the fuck out my office and don't you mention this to anybody Cali, or I'ma kill you!" Johnny threatened. After all, Johnny was the king pin over Detroit. If any word got out he was gay, he would be decapitated in a heartbeat.

"Cali!" Don yelled, chasing after Cali as she ran to the bathroom losing her stomach. Tears flowed down her eyes as she hurled over the toilet. Don was still in the hallway pacing back and forth, waiting for Cali to come back out, but she never did. She escaped out the bathroom window and ran as if her life depended on it. It was still raining outside, but Cali didn't give a damn about the rain. She needed to get to the hospital ASAP.

"Ma'am, are you alright?" a good Samaritan called out to Cali as she ran in the rain with no shoes on. He thought she was crazy and needed help, so he asked. Cali needed to call someone, and that someone was Delano. She wasn't sure if his old number was the same, but she dialed it anyway.

"Sir, do you have a phone?" Cali asked, panting like a dog that was thirsty. The good Samaritan gave her his phone to use and she dialed

Delano. He answered on the third ring. Despite their differences, he agreed to pick her up. "Thank you so much," Cali said, thanking the man as she waited inside the gas station on Grinnell and Vandyke. Although that gas station was a scary place, she stayed there waiting on Delano to pull up.

Delano pulled up in his 2020 white Lincoln Navigator, getting to Cali within 20 minutes after their call ended. Cali didn't have a coat on, just a white shirt that was covered with blood and some black jogging pants. Her honey blonde hair was clinging to her body, covering up her protruding pierced nipples.

"California, what the fuck!" Delano said, handing her a spare jacket he had in the car. He didn't want to take a chance of being an accomplice if she committed a crime and the blood be found in his truck. Plus, it was storming hard as hell outside and her titties were bouncing, making it hard for him to concentrate. "Shit, the train's coming." Delano was going north on Vandyke, not sure where he was going, and got caught by the train.

"I can't!!!!!" Cali busted into tears. She was hurt and couldn't get over the fact that her little brother was fucking her man.

"You can't what? Because you got me out here like some damn Uber," Delano complained, looking at Cali without the slightest idea of what she'd just been through. She just ignored him and bawled into tears. Her hazel eyes were now bloodshot red from all the crying. "Oh, come on now, don't do that crying shit on me." Delano parked his truck until the trained passed by, giving Cali some tissue. Even though Delano and Cali were no longer together, he still felt compassion for her. After all, they were friends, before now.

"Can you take me to St. John on Moross?" Cali requested once the train cleared. She really needed to go get tested right away. The pain in between her legs was unbearable. Most people didn't get tested once they acquired signs of a possible STD. Some didn't get tested at all, they'd rather keep fucking and spreading the disease all over. Delano nodded in agreeance, not asking why, and headed towards the hospital. "I want to join your crew. I no longer want to serve Johnny,"

Cali said out of the blue, hoping Delano wouldn't ask questions as to why she would betray her leader.

"Ok, Cali, what the fuck is really going on? You call me in the middle of the day, you got blood on your clothes, no jacket, no bra, no sho—"

"I just witnessed seven cold blooded murders and then shortly after, my brother and my man fucking. It was almost like Johnny got a thrill from killing all those innocent people," Cali answered Delano, cutting him off.

"Wait, is Johnny gay?" Delano asked. He had his suspicions when they were younger, because Johnny was cruel to women but treated men with respect. That still didn't prove much, but it was enough for Delano to know. It was that moment when Cali knew she fucked up. Johnny said not to tell anyone, or he would kill her.

"You can't tell anyone Delano. My brother is coming for your cartel soon, but I'd rather join your crew and help take Johnny out," Cali confessed, taking a cigarette from Delano's glove compartment without his permission. Delano smacked that cigarette out her hand so damn quick. She had an attitude that Delano smacked the cigarette out her hand like that.

"Don't rummage through my shit like this is yours. Besides, what makes you think I can trust you? If you could turn on your own brother, what will make me any different?" Delano pulled his gun out and pointed it at Cali's heart. "What's stopping me from killing you right now?" he asked, pressing the gun deeper into her chest.

"Because you're no killer. You only kill if necessary and you know our past will never change," Cali said, looking at Delano directly in his eyes as he pulled into St. John's emergency circular driveway.

"Alright you got my word, but the moment you think about betraying me, I will put a bullet in your heart and all three of your kids' heads," Delano threatened. He said what he said and was about his word.

"You mean all four. I have four children, but alright, we have a deal," Cali hinted, unaware how it made her look as a mother. She knew Delano didn't know about their child and he wasn't going to ask. He just looked at her confused, not allowing another word to escape his lips. He wondered what kind of mother would let her children get killed. "Ok, I will call you once I get out of here." She exited out his truck to go inside St. John's Hospital.

CALI WAITED four hours to see a doctor, taking numerous tests including blood and urine. Her nerves had her shook. She was shaking like a leaf as if she was going into shock, but she really was scared. The doctor, Marie Lavoue, finally came in and examined Cali from her waist down. The doctor extended her hand for a handshake to make Cali feel welcomed, then she began her examination. Dr. Lavoue collected samples, swabbing Cali's vagina as she laid there uncomfortable, crying silently.

"Ok honey, I'm sure the blisters are indicating you are HIV positive," she said, giving Cali her results straight without even having to run a test. "Wait, there is more. Our tests also confirm you are three weeks pregnant."

Cali jumped up covering her mouth with both of her hands. *What in the entire fuck is happening to my life?* she thought to herself, because she was at a loss for words. It was like Cali's whole world was crashing down before her. One, she didn't know who she was pregnant by, and two, she had HIV. Cali fell onto the floor screaming and crying out to Jesus. "Lord, help me!!!!"

Dr. Lavoue handed Cali her prescription and gave specific instructions. Cali's heart felt like it was shattered into pieces. She couldn't breathe nor swallow the saliva that formed in her mouth. This was the icing to the fucking cake. Cali fell off the map, no one heard from her or saw her since she left the warehouse. Delano was the last person to see Cali when he dropped her off at St. John's.

4

OH SHIT

Kairo was now spending more and more time with Delano every day. Taking mini trips across town, traveling, shopping and having meaningful sex nonstop. Those bills she had trouble with were now all paid up for the year. She didn't have to call her parents for help, nor did she have to sell her ass. Kairo really didn't even have to work anymore. Delano was taking care of her depositing $5,000 in her account every week. Her man was the fucking king pin of the south, a strip club owner and soon to take over Detroit drug market. They had just gotten back from L.A and couldn't get in the door good enough before his face was buried in Kairo's juices.

"OOOOOOOO shhhhhiiiiit, baby, right there!" Kairo moaned, tilting her head back and grinding her pussy in his face. He was eating her pussy like it was his last meal.

"Mmmmmm, damn baby, you taste so fucking good!" Delano flickered his tongue across Kairo's now swollen clit. Tightening her legs around his neck as her body began to shake uncontrollably, he was making Kairo cum multiple times, back to back, not taking a break; he just kept going. She said he was eating her pussy like it was his last meal. Delano picked Kairo up and inserted himself inside her slowly, staring her in her eyes. "Can you have my baby?" he asked, biting his bottom pink lip.

She was so fucking horny, she ended up nodding yes although she wanted the last name first. Delano held her closer to him, kissing her neck while deep stroking her. She was creaming everywhere, tightening her walls on his thickness. He sucked gently on her nipples sending chills down her spine, making her squirt while he was still inside. That drove him fucking crazy, feeling the warm juices spilling down on his rod.

"Shit girl, I love you, will you marry me?" Delano asked. Kairo didn't hesitate, she said yes. He began kissing her sloppily, increasing his strokes as he was getting near. "Oh shit baby, I'm cumming!" Delano quickened his pace as he came.

Kairo also came with him at the same time. *Did this nigga just propose to me in the middle of having sex?* Kairo thought to herself. That was some of the best dick she'd had in her whole entire 26 years of living.

They both got up and took a hot shower to clean up for dinner. Delano had his chefs prepare an extravagant dinner for them that night. He was planning on ending things with Nikki because he had serious feelings for Kairo. This was going to be a problem because he had not told either woman about the dinner.

"What is it you have to tell me?" Kairo kept asking, watching Delano's body language change because he was so uncomfortable. Next thing she knew, a petite, light-skinned woman wearing a blue sundress entered in the room.

"Babe, I'm back." She paused, looking Kairo up and down. "Who the fuck is this bitch?" she asked, dropping her shopping bags.

"Bitch?" Kairo questioned, coming out her shoes. "Who the fuck are you calling a bitch?" She had Kairo fucked up. She didn't talk shit, she handled hers.

"Ladies, calm down." Delano was now standing between them so that they couldn't hit each other.

"Why the fuck is this bitch in our house Delano?" Nikki asked in a high-pitched tone, as if she was going to cry.

"Nikki, chill," Delano said, holding on to her because she began wildly swinging her arms. Long as that bitch didn't come for Kairo swinging, she was good. It wasn't Kairo's fault her nigga lied about her. Matter of fact, he didn't even mention her.

"Why are you telling me to chill, are you fucking that bitch?" She was trying her hardest to get past him, but he wouldn't let her go.

"Since you gone keep calling me a bitch, I'm gone come show you what this bitch can do!" Kairo leaped over Delano's shoulders and punched her directly in the eye.

"Ouch, she fucking hit me!" she screamed, holding onto her eye that was going to turn black any minute now.

"Well that's what the fuck you get! Don't bring a gun to the fight if you not gone shoot, hoe!" Kairo said still rowdy, ready to whoop this boney bitch's ass. The hood Kairo was from, they didn't play that. If you gone talk shit you better know how to use them hands. She took her dress off so Nikki wouldn't have shit to grip and her hair was already in a ponytail. Kairo wasn't afraid to knock a bitch back to Africa whether she had clothes on or not. To be honest, she'd rather fight bitches naked so they had nothing to grip on. She was squaring up with bitches like she was in a boxing match.

"Both of you chill the fuck out!!" Delano said, holding his hands out to keep both women apart from each other. He really was not getting a thrill from this, but he didn't know Kairo had that in her.

Nikki lunged but missed, then Delano saw they weren't listening to him and moved out the way. It was now fair game. Kairo and Nikki went for what they knew and ended up outside falling into the pool. That didn't stop shit. They still were fighting until Delano jumped into the pool to pull them apart.

"ALRIGHT, THAT IS ENOUGH, BOTH OF YOU!" Delano yelled, stopping both women from killing each other.

"Fuck you Delano!!!!" Kairo screamed, getting out of the pool and pulling what was left of her strip lashes off. He couldn't imagine losing Kairo like this, especially when she could be pregnant with his child right now. He chased right after her, draping the towel around her naked body.

"Kairo, wait, I didn't want this to happen this way. You have to understand—"

"I don't have to understand shit!!! Get the fuck off me Delano." Kairo pushed him away, she was pissed. She tried to storm out of Delano's presence, but he kept following her.

"I want to choose you. We just share a son together, that's all." Delano was looking at her with his sorry ass. He knew he was wrong, leading Kairo on this whole time and had a family. A typical Detroit hood nigga.

"You wanted this to happen, lead me on to just hurt me. You're not stuck; you are fucking stupid," Kairo ranted and walked away. She left Delano standing in his driveway watching her pull away, and that was the last time they spoke.

TWO MONTHS LATER...

It'd been almost two months since Kairo last saw and spoke to Delano. She got herself back into the gym, using her bachelor's degree to land her a job at Beaumont as an RN. She even repaired broken relationships with her sisters and parents. Although she walked away, Delano still deposited $5,000 in her account faithfully every week. That was more than enough to keep the bills paid, while she continued to work on herself and get her finances in order.

Kairo was heading to the gym before her shift at Beaumont. She pulled over on Eight Mile just before getting to Woodward, opened the car door and BLLLAAAT! All her breakfast food came up at once. She wiped her mouth and proceeded straight to work instead. She knew she missed her period last month but wanted to be sure if she was pregnant or not. So, she scheduled a pregnancy test with her head gynecologist at work and found out she was indeed six weeks pregnant. Kairo didn't know whether to be excited or not. She knew Delano would be there for his child, but she didn't plan on being a single mother.

Once Kairo went on break, she called Cali just to see if she would answer because she hadn't heard from her in months. It seemed like

51

she fell from the face of the. They both spoke and agreed to meet at Starters after Kairo's shift ended. She was excited to see her friend, but she was in for a total surprise.

After Kairo's shift ended at 7 pm, she went straight to Starter's downtown since she was already on Thirteen Mile and Woodward. She sat there 30 minutes, waiting on Cali, before she ordered her entree. Listening to the Motown songs Starter's had in rotation, sipping on her lemon water.

Cali finally arrived stumbling off the Q-Line, after Kairo waited damn near an hour for her to show. Kairo hadn't seen Cali in months and she was in a bad place. Her hair was matted, and her skin was pale with no pigmentation whatsoever.

She had lost so much weight that Kairo was able to notice her baby bump that looked like she was about three months. Once Cali approached the table, the foul stench from her clothes made Kairo silently gag, but Kairo kept a straight face. Despite the smell, Kairo got up, extended her arms out to hug her, and they both sat down.

"Hey girl, where the hell you been?" Kairo excitedly asked, watching Cali's body language. She didn't crack a smile, she just kept fidgeting her clothes. Kairo didn't even want to tell her the good news about her being pregnant, she was more concerned about her friend.

"Do you have any money?" Cali asked coldly. She didn't even address the fact Kairo just asked her a question. Cali was badly using drugs, three months pregnant and things were just getting worse day by day.

"No, I don't have any money," Kairo lied, shaking her head no. "What's wrong?" She reached out her hands across the wooden table, touching Cali's hands that were shaking nonstop. She was acting nervous and weird. Kairo didn't know these were the normal signs of a drug addict, because she was never exposed to that community. Cali was hurting and had no one to run and talk to. She didn't feel right talking to Kairo, because Kairo was the partial reason.

"Please, I need to take the Q- Line back home. I'm staying at a women's shelter," Cali begged for money, but had other intentions on what to use it for. Kairo wasn't dumb, she needed to know if she was using drugs.

"Cali are you using drugs? Please be hon—"

"Bitch, does it look like I'm using drugs?" Cali cut into Kairo from asking her a question. She was offended by what was obvious. Kairo was shocked at Cali for snapping at her like that. All she wanted to do was look out for her friend, but Cali made it difficult.

"Whoa, all I want to do is help you. Would you like me to drop you off home?"

"No, I can find my own way home. I don't need your bougie ass doing shit for me," Cali responded in an offensive tone. "You think you're better than me? You ain't shit Kairo!"

Now Kairo squinted her eyes at her, trying to make out what Cali was saying. "What! Where the fuck did that come from Cali?" Kairo asked, still watching Cali pull up her sleeves revealing her arms that were covered with sores. "Cali, what the fuck, are you on drugs?" Kairo stated again, reaching out to grab her arms.

"No, bitch, does it look like I'm on fucking drugs to you?" Cali snapped again, snatching her arms off the table. Her eyes that used to be bright and hazel were now dim and bloodshot red with dark circles around her eye sockets. Cali was in denial; she didn't give a damn about anything else. She wanted some damn cocaine and heroin.

"You know you can talk to me, tell me what's going on." Kairo tried reaching for Cali's hands across the table once more. Cali pulled her hands back, still scratching her arms. She was having withdrawals and wanted a hit. She just knew Kairo had some money, that's why she met her at Starter's.

"Bitch, I'm not telling you shit!" Cali prevailed, taking Kairo's lemon water and splashing it in her face. Kairo paused, closed her eyes while the water dripped down her face. She was contemplating on jumping across the table to beat Cali's ass, but decided not to. Cali's true colors were now starting to show, but Kairo knew this wasn't her friend. The drugs had to be getting her off her rockers. She didn't even react to Cali's outburst or the fact she threw water in her face. She just politely got up, putting the money in the hands of the waitress for Cali's meal, and left a hefty tip.

Kairo was saddened for her friend. She needed help, but she wasn't going to force her. This was something Cali had to do on her own. All Kairo could do was walk away. She wasn't familiar to the drugs Cali was using but she could remember losing all four of her oldest brothers to drugs. Drug overdose took them out the game before they could reach 30.

THE FOLLOWING MORNING, Kairo got up and got dressed for her family planning appointment at Planned Parenthood on Cass Ave. Yesterday, after finding out she was with child, she scheduled a 12 pm appointment. She thought to call her parents and sisters to share the news, but she wasn't sure whether she was going to keep the baby or not. She had two options, either she could terminate her pregnancy or give it up for adoption. She hadn't decided which one yet. Hopefully, she could reach a decision soon or one was going to be made for her.

Kairo was feeling dreadful that morning, so she played "It Kills Me" by Melanie Fiona while warm tears fell into the palms of her hands. She missed Delano. It was crazy he didn't call, he didn't even reach out to her. The only thing he did was deposit money into her account. Finding out she was pregnant made things worse, because here it was she was deciding on what she was going to do with their baby without him being there.

"Ooh, I've got to be outta my mind, to think it's going to work this time. A part of me wants to leave but the other side still believes. Ooh and it kills me, to know how much, how much I really LOOOOVVVE you," Kairo recited the lyrics verbatim, feeling the words that escaped her lips. The neighbors next door to her knocked on the walls, because Kairo was too loud.

"SHUT THE FUCK UP!!!!" the neighbor shouted, startling Kairo who had snot and tears intertwined. She was sick of these motherfuckas getting over. She didn't pay all that money for someone to tell her to shut the fuck up, so she took her broom and walked next door.

"BITCH, FUCK YOU! YOU MISERABLE ASS CUNT!!" Kairo screamed, pounding on their door with her broom, creating dents each time she thwacked. They pissed her the fuck off and she was ready to take somebody's head off. They turned their music up to drown out the loud banging Kairo was causing. "YEA, KEEP THAT NEGATIVE SHIT IN YOUR CONDO! I don't pay $1500 a month for a mothafucka to tell me to shut the fuck up," Kairo spazzed and returned to her apartment. She had to get the fuck out of there before they called the police. She put her coat on and walked out the door.

Walking towards her truck, she noticed the gigantic word HOME-WRECKER in white spray paint all over the driver's side. Whoever this was also had the nerve to key her doors so deep you would think a T-Rex existed. Kairo could smell what appeared to be human shit smeared all over the windows. She snatched the white envelope that was taped to her windshield, and inside was a note that read, *Bitch, you are a homewrecker! He will never love you, you pathetic, weak bitch!*

When Kairo finished reading the note, she looked up and saw a red Camaro speeding towards her trying to take her out the game, but Kairo was quicker than that. She saw Nikki as she was speeding by in that same car Kairo had noticed was following her these past couple of days.

"Oh hell no, I know this bitch wasn't that stupid!" Kairo said, jumping inside her badly damaged truck. She was already on 10 from her neighbors fucking with her earlier. Kairo shifted her car into drive following behind Nikki. Although it was impossible to see with smeared shit everywhere, it was nothing windshield wipers and fluid couldn't wipe away. Kairo was ready to rip someone's head off, fuck that 12 o'clock appointment. Nikki didn't know she just opened a can of whoop ass.

Kairo and Nikki were speeding up Gratiot cutting through traffic, moving rapidly through red lights, fuck the law at this point. Nikki didn't care. Nikki knew she'd fucked up when she looked in her rearview mirror and she saw Kairo on her ass. HOONK, HOONK, HOOOONK! Kairo blew her horn. She was madder than a mother-fucka. This bitch was about to leave her son motherless. Kairo was so close on Nikki's ass her truck tapped the bumper of her Camaro, sending her to lose control of the car. Her car spun and landed on the opposite side of Seven Mile and Gratiot by the Citi Trends.

Kairo's adrenaline was pumping. She didn't give a fuck if Nikki was hurt or not. She purposely ran her truck right into Nikki's passenger side causing more damage. Nikki was about to learn a lesson today, not to fuck with Kairo or her truck. Bystanders were now gathering around pulling out their camera phones to record the drama.

"Bitch, get your ass out the fucking car. You want to fuck up my truck, I'm gone fuck you up!" Kairo yelled, cutting her hands on the shards of glass. She was trying to retrieve her baseball bat from the trunk. Nikki just stayed in the car, calling whoever she was on the phone with. While Kairo took the baseball bat and went crazy busting the windows out, Nikki was steady in the car screaming.

Kairo was dragging this bitch out of her Camaro into the middle of Seven Mile. Her freshly manicured nails sunk deep into Nikki's skin, and Kairo used all her strength like she was the Incredible Hulk dragging Nikki into the parking lot of McDonald's. Her skin was now being scraped and she was bleeding as her skin came in contact on the street pavement.

"Bitch, let me go!!" Nikki shrieked, kicking wildly, but Kairo had her in a firm hold.

"No, you brought this on yourself, so now deal with it!" Kairo was punching Nikki in the face.

They were fighting like two bitches in the street. Then Nikki picked up Kairo's bat attempting to hit Kairo with it, but she caught it mid swing and yanked it out her hand. Soon as Kairo took the bat to turn and use it on Nikki, the police officer stopped her just in time.

"Who's the stupid bitch now?" Kairo yelled as she was being pulled away in handcuffs.

"You still the stupid bitch, getting handcuffed and going to jail." Nikki laughed with blood running down her nose. While Nikki was talking mad shit, she was also going to jail. The officer put Kairo and Nikki in separate squad cars, escorting them to the ninth precinct on

Gratiot. They were fingerprinted and tossed into separate holding cells.

Officer Tomlin came to ask Kairo's side of the story first and why she was so hostile at the accident. She went on to tell the officer that she was on her way to her doctor's appointment when Nikki vandalized her truck and tried to run her over with her car. That was enough to press charges for endangerment of an unborn child and aggravated assault.

Then, Kairo overheard Jimenez talking to the officers in front. He was posting bail for Kairo and Nikki, but Nikki's charges were more of a serious offense, so bail couldn't be posted for her. Delano must have known Kairo and Nikki got into an altercation. Then Nikki saw Jimenez and waved, signaling him to come over.

"My apologies, Nikki, but Delano assigned me to Kairo," he said, walking over to Kairo's cell. Nikki's face expression turned from excitement to disappointment.

"Oh, hell no!! How you gone represent that bitch?" Nikki scoffed.

Jimenez ignored her and turned towards Kairo. He told her Delano sent him to get her out of jail, and that he broke things off with Nikki the same day Kairo left him. Nikki was having trouble letting go, which explained the harassment that was taking place. Jimenez also pulled out a note and gave it to Kairo to read.

Dear Kairo,

I know you are mad at me, but I still choose you. Please forgive me and let's be friends. –

Delano.

"WELL CAN you take me to Delano?" Kairo asked. She'd made up her mind to go see him. She wanted to talk to him in person so she could know if he left Nikki for herself. Jimenez nodded and escorted Kairo to Asbury Park.

They pulled up to Asbury Park within 30 minutes after leaving the police station. It was kind of chilly outside in the fall, so the leaves were turning red and falling onto the ground. Delano was there playing basketball with a crew of men without his shirt on. The sweat from his body glistened over his six-pack chest exposing his tribal tattoo on his left arm. Kairo was getting turned on just from watching him sweat. After all, it'd been two months since she last saw him, so her hormones were racing like a racehorse.

"Hola, mi amor!" Delano yelled, waving across the court jogging over to Kairo. He was so happy to see her; he couldn't wait to be in her presence. He hugged her so tightly that she could barely breathe. Kairo felt his dick jumping through his grey Nike shorts; he really was excited to see her. "First off, I want to apologize for the damage done to your truck. I already have your truck in the shop getting repaired as we speak." Delano grabbed Kairo's hands. She was impressed with how quickly he handled her situation.

"I appreciate all that you have done. I know we haven't gotten along—"

"Shhh! Kairo, I meant everything I said. I intend to protect and love you, if you just let me," Delano interrupted her as he took Kairo's badly wrapped hand and held it close to his heart while looking her in the eyes. She felt that he was being honest with her but wasn't sure entirely.

"I believe you, but I can't help but wonder what happens next?" Kairo questioned, because she felt like she was being played to the left.

"What do you mean what happens next? Come sit down with me and let's talk." Delano was putting his white tee shirt back over his head, sitting down on the park bench. He tapped the bench signaling for her to sit down. Kairo had her wall up as she sat next to Delano, folding her arms across her chest. She didn't even want to look at him, her mood changed just that fast.

"What are you going to do about Nikki and your son?" Kairo asked, turning her body towards Delano. She wasn't interested in coming second to any bitch. It was either her or Nikki. One of them must go. She wasn't about to settle for being anyone's side chick. If he chose her, she would have to get used to having his son around. Delano licked his lips before responding.

"If you are asking me who I'm choosing to spend the rest of my life with, I choose you." Delano touched the bottom of Kairo's face to gain her full attention. "I was on the verge of ending things with Nikki that night, that's why I had that extravagant dinner. I fucked up when I misinformed both of you. Again, I apologize again for what she's done. She's just salty from me moving out and selling the house."

"Wait, you moved out? Then where is your son?" Kairo questioned, because Nikki was still locked up for aggravated assault, facing time for prison for attempted murder, and he was with her at the park.

"Nikki called me and told me she got into a scuffle with you and she left him with her house servants. Besides all that, are you ready to take our relationship to another level?" Delano expressed. He wasted no time telling Kairo he wanted to continue the relationship with her.

"Well first off, I forgive you, and yes I'm ready for the next level, but there's something I need to tell you first," Kairo confessed. She had mixed emotions telling him about the baby after all that she endured with Nikki and Cali trying to get at her over him.

"Ok, what is it?" Delano asked, smiling at Kairo. He already knew what she was going to say.

"I'm pregnant!" Kairo said excitedly. Delano's smile quickly turned into a big ass Kool-Aid smile. He already knew she was pregnant, and all that time she was away, he spent time trying to get prepared for the baby.

"I already knew that, that's why I'm prepared to give you this." Delano reached in his pocket and handed Kairo a pair of keys wrapped in a pretty pink ribbon. Delano was also a provider. He made sure all his women were taken care of. He wanted to get Kairo out the hood and move her into something bigger.

"What is this for?" Kairo asked, curious as to what those keys went to.

"The first step to showing you that I'm serious about us. I'm getting you and the baby out the city and putting us in a bigger house. The second pair of keys is to your rental until your truck gets out the shop," Delano said, getting on his knees to kiss Kairo's stomach.

Delano's phone began to ring suddenly. He looked at the screen and his facial expression immediately changed. "My bad babe, something came up at the club and I need to go check it out real quick. Jimenez is going to take you to our new home. I will meet you there."

"Alright, I will see you later." Kairo kissed him goodbye before parting ways.

AFTER DRIVING for what felt like forever, Jimenez and Kairo finally pulled into a long driveway. It took them 10 minutes before reaching the actual property. This house was a mansion bigger than her parents' house in the Indian Village. She took her keys and entered, the smell of fresh paint filling her nostrils. She could tell the house was newly built from the paint on the walls and the black glossy floors. This was no ordinary house, this was a mansion—3,580 sq. ft. to be exact, five bedrooms, four bathrooms, a movie theater in the basement, and a two-in-one pool.

"Welcome Mrs. Harris, can I take you to the master's room?" The maid who went by the name Rose, like the champagne, escorted Kairo up to the master's room. Kairo was confused as to why she called her Mrs. Harris and they weren't married yet. Delano already had it set up and told his staff to call her Mrs. Harris, for she would soon have his last name. As Kairo walked into the room, she noticed on the bed were gifts from her favorite stores, MAC, Dior, Gucci, Tiffany and Co. and many more.

"Ok, this is a beautiful room, but where the fuck is the ceiling?" Kairo asked Rose, because every room had a ceiling but this one. She didn't know Delano designed the whole mansion. She thought it was built wrong with a missing ceiling.

"I'm sorry, you have a glass ceiling that's sound and shatter proof Mrs. Harris. With the click of this button, the ceiling will change to metal, if you ever want pure darkness. Mr. Harris designed this house and had it built from the ground up," Rose said. As she was showing Kairo the button on the wall that was hidden, Kairo thought to herself, she had one talented, fine ass man.

"So, where are the lights?" Kairo asked because she didn't see them. Normally they would be on the ceiling.

"They are in the walls, see." Rose clicked on the lights. "Would you like to see the baby room?"

"Baby room?" Kairo questioned. She was not expecting a maternity room to be set up, but with Delano it seemed like he was always prepared.

"Yes, Mr. Harris said there will be a baby soon. With this button you will be able to enter the baby room." Rose clicked another button and the room shifted, and the baby room was visible. This mansion was some futuristic ass shit. Kairo swore no other house was engineered like this. Suddenly, Kairo and Rose were startled by Jimenez rushing up the stairs. He was out of breath holding his heart like he'd been shot.

"I'm sorry Kairo, something terrible has happened at the club," Jimenez said, panicking, now making her panic because she hadn't heard anything from Delano in over two hours.

"WHAT!!!" she screamed, dialing Delano's number and getting voicemail. "Jimenez, where is he?" Kairo asked, trying to control her emotions. Her head was getting light and her body was getting hot.

"He's been shot multiple times. We don't know if he will be able to make it," Jimenez said with a tremble in his voice, holding back his tears. Jimenez tried to console Kairo as much as he could, but she broke out of his arms.

"Oh hell no! Don't say that!!!" Kairo screamed, grabbing the keys to the rental, rushing down all 35 stairs, and jumping in the car. She pulled out so fast, she didn't even notice Jimenez followed behind her. It was raining hard as hell, but she didn't give a fuck about rain. She was still speeding up I-75 trying to get to Delano.

She knew not to drive fast in the rain but she wasn't thinking straight. All she was thinking about was getting to her man to make sure he was alive. Jimenez then sped up on Kairo's car cutting her car off, sending her car to come to sudden stop. SSSSCUUUUUR-RRRRRRRRRRTT! Kairo's car spun out of control causing her car to hit the concrete wall.

5

TRAGIC LOSS

Kairo's ears had a high pitch ringing noise as she slowly regained consciousness. She tried to unfasten her seatbelt but realized she was trapped inside the car that was split into two, upside down. She wasn't sure how long she'd been out for, but it couldn't have been for too long because she suddenly remembered why she was speeding. Kairo had blood leaking onto her face as she noticed the blood soiling her clothes but was unable to detect where from.

She tried moving but she was too weak. She was still determined to find him. Kairo felt he needed her there by his side during a time like this. "Help!! Help!!" Kairo weakly screamed for help, but no one was there to hear her. Then shortly the EMS pulled up with flashing lights rushing over to her, using the Jaws of Life to cut her out.

"Ma'am! Can you hear me?" the EMT asked, to see if she was still alive. Although they were right next to her, their voices sounded muffled and distant. She was so weak she could feel herself slipping in and out of consciousness.

"Help!" Kairo called out again before passing out. The EMT hooked her up to a ventilator to help her breathe and escorted her to Receiving Hospital. When Kairo awoke, she was laid on a stretcher in the hospital with all types of tubes running into her skin. "Delano!!!"

Kairo screamed, getting the attention of the nurses as she was pulling the needles out her veins, causing herself to bleed.

"Ma'am, calm down, we almost have you admitted," the nurse said, reinserting the IV into her veins. Kairo was still fighting the woman because she didn't like needles. The nurse remained calm while Kairo wrestled with her.

"Ma'am, please relax, we need to stabilize you," the nurse said, taking Kairo's blood pressure. She wasn't hearing shit the nurse had to say, she needed to get to Delano. Kairo kept trying to escape but the nurses weren't having that. "Ma'am, we will have to give you a chill pill if you don't stop acting crazy right this minute," the nurse threatened.

"Please, I need to find my boyfriend. You don't understand, he is out here all alone," Kairo pleaded to the nurse hoping she could understand, but again, it wasn't her job to understand. She just continued to examine Kairo carefully from the blood that soiled her clothes. She discovered she was pregnant and was experiencing an early miscarriage.

"I'm sorry you are experiencing this, but we need to get you into urgent surgery." The nurse grabbed Kairo's hand and rushed her into immediate surgery. Kairo wailed in tears because she had just lost her baby from all this stress caused today. She only just found out yesterday she was pregnant. So, she really didn't have the chance to decide a name or get to experience her first pregnancy. Kairo felt like she lost everything all within 24 hours, her friend, her baby, and her boyfriend. If they hadn't rushed her to surgery to remove the fetus, she would have died as well.

"Ma'am, I'm Maria, your nurse for tonight," Maria said, coming into the room after the surgery, writing her name and number on the white board.

"Please Maria, I need to make a phone call or two," Kairo said weakly. Maria nodded her head and brought the phone to Kairo. She dialed Delano's cell again and still got voicemail. Next, she called Jimenez to see if he'd heard anything on Delano's whereabouts, and he said he didn't know anything. She didn't even tell him she was involved in an accident; she just didn't know that he was the one to cause it. Right before Jimenez ran her off the road, he received a phone call from someone giving him specific instructions. He did exactly what he was told, and it worked successfully. Finally, Kairo called her parents since she needed someone there with her.

Kairo had one rough ass day. She went to jail for dragging bitches in the middle of Seven Mile, her boyfriend was missing, she lost the baby and had this unexpected ass car accident. *How unfortunate, all this shit happens like this in one day?* Kairo thought to herself as she laid on the hospital bed, uncomfortable from the surgery.

"Ma'am, can you tell me your name so that we can contact your relatives?" Maria asked, writing on her clipboard. Kairo struggled to give her information, because she was under a lot of distress from the surgery.

"But I already contacted my relatives," Kairo said, holding her hand up to her head because she had a bad migraine from the lighting in the room. Maria saw the distress Kairo was under and told her to rest and she would be back to check on her within an hour. Soon as Kairo closed her eyes, two knocks on the door startled her. Kairo's mother came in and closed the door. Her mother resembled Phylicia Rashad off *The Cosby Show*. That's where Kairo got most of her good looks, from her strong, intelligent mother.

"Hey Mommy!" Kairo said with tears in my eyes. She was ashamed of her mother even seeing her like this. Badly dinged up in the hospital, wrapped with bandages.

"Hey, my precious peach," her mother said as she came closer to hug Kairo. "Why haven't you called us in so long? We had to find out you were pregnant though the news," her mother said, now pulling up a chair next to Kairo's bed. Kairo wondered how her mother found out she was pregnant and from what news. She didn't recall seeing Channel 4, 2 or 7.

"Mom, what news? And I'm just finding out I was pregnant myself," Kairo said emotionally, thinking about the baby and Delano.

"Some man named Jimenez called us and told us you were in an accident. Do you know who that is?" Kairo's mother asked. Kairo just nodded her head yes. Something fishy was going on. She didn't recall telling Jimenez she was pregnant, or that she was in an accident. Kairo's mother saw the look on Kairo's face and decided to change the subject. "Well your father is at the church with some of the others interceding on your behalf that you may be healed." She reached her hand out towards Kairo and started praying, speaking in tongues. Kairo just laid there praying with her, staring up into the ceiling. "You are covered with the blood of Jesus. Even though you are in your sin, God still has a plan for you," her mother said, hoping she would repent and live right.

"Mother, I thank you for coming but I really need to rest now," Kairo said, giving her mother the hint she wanted to be alone. She understood and kissed Kairo's forehead and left to go back to the church. Kairo closed her eyes finally for a few minutes and woke back up when Maria came barging into the room. Kairo's instincts told her to watch Maria. She was sneaky, rambling through the cabinets looking for something. Maria didn't even knock or acknowledge Kairo before she came into the room.

Kairo laid there, watching her as she was filling a syringe with clear liquid that she pulled from her pocket. Kairo quickly removed the IV out her arm discreetly and picked up a pan with her waste and waited until Maria got close before she made a move.

"This is for Johnny BIIITTC—" Maria said, turning around rushing at Kairo full force. Kairo threw her piss directly in Maria's face, stopping her from coming near. Kairo leaped out the bed grabbing Maria and twisted her arm behind her back.

"How much money is he paying you to kill me?" Kairo asked, holding her in a choke hold, twisting her arm a little further.

"Bitch, fuck you, ahhhh!" she yelped in pain.

"Keep on insulting me and you will not be breathing. Now TELL ME HOW MUCH!!!" Kairo yelled in her ear, hoping it would intimidate her.

"$50k to whoever kills you first!" Maria said as Kairo snatched the syringe out her hand, jabbing it into her neck. Kairo watched her lifeless body fall to the floor before leaving. She wanted to be sure that bitch Maria died instantly. So she checked her pulse and got nothing.

Kairo got out of there, removing Maria's work badge and car keys from her pocket. She wasn't sure which car was Maria's so she walked out still in her hospital gown, bleeding, until she got to the employee garage. She hit her keypad to reveal which car was the Ford Focus and drove over to The Black Stallion to find Delano.

Once Kairo finally reached the club, it looked as if it'd been abandoned for years. Kairo walked into a fucking massacre like she was in Silent Hill. Glass was shattered from the gunshots, blood splattered all over and the feathers from the cushions were flying around like snow. Yet no bodies had been found. She searched the whole club from top to bottom. Not once did she stop searching for him. "Where the fuck is Delano?" Kairo asked herself. She was having such a bad time right now she felt as if she was in a *Nightmare on Elm St*. She needed to get home. She was now bleeding profusely through the hospital gown. Before Kairo could reach the car, she was so weak from losing blood she collapsed at the entrance of the club.

"KAIRO!" she heard a familiar voice calling her while she was unconscious. She also heard distant chatter in the background. Kairo woke up and tried adjusting her eyes from the bright lights that were beaming down on her face. She looked around and noticed she was in a strange white room with no windows. Jimenez and two other Hispanic men were in the room along with her. She didn't know who they were, so she jumped up, afraid, catching Jimenez's attention.

"Oh, thank God, you're alive," Jimenez said, rushing over to Kairo's bedside. She had this enormous headache that was so overbearing she couldn't muster any words to say. She had to hold her head as she sat up in the bed trying to gain strength.

"Who the fuck are they?" Kairo questioned, pointing at the two strange men that were in her room.

"That's Julio Mendoza and Juan Ramirez, the Colombians that were sent here for protection. We thought you were dead," Jimenez said, pulling up his chair.

"Hell, I went through some shit. I had a bitch trying to kill me at

Receiving Hospital, I even spoke to you," Kairo said, looking at Jimenez. Mendoza and Ramirez both looked at Kairo strangely and then towards each other. "Why the fuck y'all looking at each other like that?" she asked because she was confused.

"Kairo, you've been in a coma for three weeks now. I found your car on I-75 after I left behind you," Jimenez confessed, telling the partial truth. He was the one that caused the accident. Kairo knew she wasn't going crazy. *He is playing with me*, she thought to herself.

"Oh hell no, now you are lying, and Delano?" Kairo asked, because maybe the part about him being shot was also a part of the dream, but that part was real. Delano was set up to get killed that night.

"He is safe, we sent him to New Orleans to see the Voodoo queen to heal him, and she sent a special elixir for you to have vivid dreams as reality to keep your brain active. It required a sacrifice though," Jimenez said, handing Kairo a cup of ice-cold water.

"Who the fuck is this Voodoo queen? And what sacrifice? Jimenez, I swear I will get out this bed and slap some sense into you!" Kairo threatened him. She didn't believe in Voodoo. He was bullshitting talking about some damn Voodoo queen.

"Ay, no need to be hostile. We're all fucked up over this," Jimenez said, putting his hands up.

"Take me to Delano right now!" Kairo demanded, but Jimencz prevailed.

"I'm afraid I won't be able to do that, he's still under," Jimenez said, standing up to walk out the room.

"Are fucking you kidding me? That's when he needs me the most. We already lost our baby, so I'm not about to let him go through this alone," Kairo said, finding the strength to stand on her feet. "Take me to see him now." Kairo wanted to be by her man's side, no matter what the situation was, she still wanted to be there.

It wasn't long before Jimenez and Kairo boarded Delano's private helicopter taking them two and a half hours to reach their destination. The sky was dark grey, and the sun was nowhere to be found. It was almost like a dangerous storm was headed their way. This weather was nothing like Kairo's experience up north. She didn't know what to expect but she hoped it passed over. They experienced a bit of turbulence from the strong winds, but it was nearly enough to take them under.

They landed safely in the middle of the plains, and shortly after, a black man dressed in overalls and a straw hat met Kairo and Jimenez. He transported them to the Voodoo queen in a busted down raggedy rover that was faster than an average streetcar. The man that transported them smelt badly like he reeked of death, making it difficult for Kairo and Jimenez to breathe. Kairo's nostrils began to sting from this man's stench, making her vomit.

Finally, passing through the swamps and into the bayou, they reached their destination where Delano was staying. Kairo was happy to find him. It didn't matter what condition he was in, whether he was dead or alive. Just as long as she was with him again. Kairo entered a small hut that was covered in tall grass and mud, and Jimenez followed behind. The smell of dead flesh was the normal aroma. Delano was laid on a table surrounded by all kinds of spices and herbs. An elder woman was wiping mud off his body speaking another language Kairo didn't know.

"Come in my child, don't you be afraid," she spoke in English as Kairo crept into the room. "I need you to come here. I've been expecting you." The woman held her hands out. Kairo walked near her, standing next to Delano, and she took Kairo's hand in her hand.

"Ouch, what the fuck woman?!" Kairo screamed as the Voodoo queen cut open her palm, placing it on Delano's heart. His heartbeat was weak until the blood from Kairo's hand touched his chest.

"He needs you Kairo. Before you came his heart was decreasing day by day. Eventually, he would have died in his human form. The bullets struck multiple nerves and he should have been paralyzed, but since he was rushed to me I was able to save him," the Voodoo queen said as she spread the same mud off his body into Kairo's bloody palm.

"What do you mean died in his human form?" Kairo asked, curious as to what she meant by human form.

"If I had to do the ritual to bring him back to life, he would never be the same, he would be possessed by a demon. Then he would constantly smell of death making it impossible for you to ever be intimate. Magic always comes with a price, the ultimate sacrifice," the Voodoo queen said washing the mud away. Kairo's hand was restored back to normal as if she never cut it. "I need you to speak life to him, and when he wakes give him this elixir, the same one you drank."

Kairo stood next to Delano and bawled into tears, she hated to see him like this. Kairo began telling him how much she loved him and slowly, little by little, his body responded. Her tears dropped onto his skin as she planted warm kisses all over his face. Delano's eyes slowly began to open, and he took a long inhale of air before he started coughing up blood.

"Give him the elixir now!" the Voodoo queen shouted. Kairo immediately gave him the elixir and he drank it quickly.

"Whoa, what the fuck was that shit?!" Delano said, twisting his face up looking at the blue bottle.

"That was to kill any viruses or infections that manifested in your body during the ritual," the Voodoo queen said, handing Delano a bucket to vomit in. "There will be no transferring of demonic spirits in Delano, the ritual is now complete."

"You said all magic comes with a price, a sacrifice. What was our sacrifice?" Kairo asked.

"Your first child was the sacrifice. It was meant for you to get into that accident so that Delano could live. Don't worry, you will have two more to replace the one you've lost," she said, touching Kairo's shoulder as she grabbed her stomach.

"Thank you, Queen," Delano said as he signaled Jimenez to bring her the 100k, but the Voodoo queen refused.

"No family of mine has to pay for any of this Voodoo healing, you've already lost enough. Now get back north, you have a war to win," she said before snapping her fingers, returning to her youthful self, disappearing right in front of their eyes. Kairo had never seen any shit like that in her entire life. Voodoo was real and it happened right here in New Orleans, Louisiana.

On the way back home, Kairo held Delano's warm hand.

"Hey baby, I love you with all my heart," Delano said, kissing her hand.

"I love you too," Kairo responded, laying her head on his warm chest. She wanted to kill Johnny, decapitate him and put his head on a fucking stick. Burn his body, letting the crows eat it! He was not going to get away with this. He was going to pay for every single thing.

6

WAR ZONE

SIX MONTHS LATER...

"Ahhhhh, shit baby!" Delano moaned as he woke up to Kairos's tight lips wrapped around his extremely rock-hard erection. The sunlight beamed down in their room as she deep throated his dick so perfectly, with no teeth, making slurping and gagging noises. His eyes still were closed as he enjoyed every bit of Kairo's warm mouth, holding her head close to throat fuck her. Delano was so turned on by the way Kairo was doing her tongue tricks he had a quick eruption. Normally Kairo would swallow, but today she wanted to watch his shit explode.

"Damn baby, I love when you cum!" she moaned, licking up the mess Delano just made in their king-size California bed. He turned Kairo over and inserted himself inside her warm, tight pussy. Her shit gripped his dick like a small rubber band you put around your wrist, her pussy was just that tight. Although they fucked every day, Kairo's pussy still was tight like the first time, and Delano wasn't even her first. He smacked both ass cheeks watching her arch deeper so he could bury all eight inches inside.

"Fuck! I love this good pussy," Delano groaned, slowing up his pace as her pussy dripped cream down his balls and legs. Kairo creamed so much you'd think it was a cream pie, but it was all her. She reached an orgasm, but Delano still wasn't done. She turned on her back and he hungrily started sucking her nipples, increasing speed as he was nearing.

"Yes daddy, fuck this pussy!" Kairo screamed and soon as she said that, Delano erupted all inside her. He collapsed in the bed with his heart beating faster than a race car, and Kairo fell on top of him lying on his chest as they watched the sunrise together. Delano leaned over to the nightstand grabbing his phone before hooking it up to the Bluetooth playing "Tribe" by Bas ft. J. Cole. He was still aroused and wanted some more, so he picked Kairo up and placed her on the wall.

Cum was still spewing from his dick from a few minutes ago, but he still stuck it inside her holding her legs over his shoulders. Delano was kissing her warm neck as she moaned softly in his ears. Delano did steady slow, circular motions inside her now swollen vagina and she squirted warm juices back on his rod. That shit made him go crazy, and he came inside her again.

"AHHHHHHH!" Delano yelped in pain as he caught a Charlie horse while he came.

"Baby what's wrong?" Kairo asked, grabbing a warm towel to clean him up.

"Fucking Charlie horse!" Delano yelled, holding on to his lower left calf. She removed the warm towel from his penis to his lower calf and massaged it with the towel relieving the Charlie horse. Delano loved this woman. She knew exactly what to do and he didn't have to ask or tell her what to do. *It's time I make her my wife and stop fucking her guts and trying to get her pregnant*, Delano thought to himself, admiring how she cared for him. Delano loved everything about her, she made him the happiest man alive.

"Any word on Johnny's whereabouts?" she asked, running a hot shower to clean herself up.

"No, I haven't heard anything. I still got the Colombians searching for him," Delano replied, joining Kairo in the shower. Since the first attack six months ago, Johnny disappeared into thin air without leaving a trace. California also was looking for him and he didn't ever leave without telling his family. Delano felt revenge was a must from the ambush against him and his men at The Black Stallion.

"What are the plans for today Mr. Harris?" Kairo asked while wrapping the towel around her naked body.

"Let's go ring shopping," Delano suggested. He'd already proposed to her during an intimate time, and he wanted to make sure she had the finest ring money could buy.

"Oh my god, baby really?" Kairo screamed. She was too excited, jumping all around the room. Delano was serious about making her his wife. So, they went and picked out one of the most expensive engagement rings from the Blue Nile collection. Listed at $50,000, an emerald-cut sapphire surrounded by a halo of pave-set diamonds in an 18k white-gold ring. Kairo was so fucking happy she couldn't stop thanking and kissing Delano.

"Let's have an engagement dinner party tonight. Can you invite your family?" Delano asked, because they been together for eight months and he had yet to meet her family. He knew her parents were pastors over at Spiritual Word of Faith here in Detroit, but that was all he knew.

"Anything you want to do," she replied before they were interrupted by a call from Jimenez. The Colombians had found Johnny and had him hidden away tied up in the basement of the club. Jimenez wanted Delano to meet them there within 30 minutes. Before he departed, Delano gave Kairo money for the supplies for tonight's party. She was so distracted by her new ring. She really wasn't paying attention to Delano's actions. He dropped Kairo back off to her truck and headed over to The Black Stallion. He didn't tell her the Colombians found Johnny to protect her from getting hurt. Delano felt like this war was between Johnny and him. Although they'd both been planning to kill him together, Johnny also wanted to kill Kairo as well. That was a risk Delano was not willing to take. He couldn't live with himself if Johnny were to kill Kairo, and that's why he had to kill Johnny first.

Delano made it to the club within the 30 minutes like Jimenez requested and went straight to the basement through the back door.

The Black Stallion Club was opened between 10 am-12 pm to the public for lunch so he didn't want to alarm his guests or staff. The Colombians already had Johnny discreetly tied up in the basement and once Delano got there, they left the room.

Delano walked into his black soundproof room, where he found Johnny tied up in a chair with a black silk bag over his head. He snatched the bag from off his head and noticed Johnny's mouth gag stuffed in his mouth. He thought about all the horrible shit Johnny did to him while he served and punched Johnny directly into his hard rib cage twice. Johnny groaned in pain as the saliva escaped his mouth from the gag. He punched him again, this time in his left eye, leaving a mark. He grabbed Johnny by the neck choking him, lifting him and the chair, looking at him in the face.

"Nigga, it was me that introduced you to this fucking life, don't get shit confused! You tried to kill me, but I'm still fucking here!" Delano yelled with veins bulging from the side of his neck.

Dropping Johnny's chair, he displayed no emotion. He knew it was only a matter of time before his men came storming in Delano's club to rescue him. Delano held his gun up to Johnny's bloody eye, then Johnny started mumbling something. Delano removed the mouth gag allowing Johnny to speak.

"Man, let's be honest, you're really mad because I found a better connect with the Italians than your weak ass Colombians." Johnny spit on the ground as a sign of disrespect against the Colombians. He hated competition, the main reason why he never gave Delano the Westside of Detroit. Johnny enjoyed being the only ruthless kingpin he was.

"Johnny, you let all this power go to your head. I should have been put a bullet in your head a long time ago." Delano took the power drill off the black table, loading it with a sharp drill bit that could tear through flesh. ZZZZZZZZZ, was the sound the drill made as he was drilling a hole deep into Johnny's right shoulder blade. Johnny's screams filled the soundproof room, as he watched his skin being distorted by a power drill.

Johnny's plan was coming right into play just as he imagined it. He knew Kairo was Delano's weakness, so he had to come out of hiding. A nigga wouldn't be found unless he wanted to be found, and Johnny had to eliminate Delano from the game. Although Kairo did owe Johnny money for missing two payments, it was Cali who suggested she be wiped out. If Johnny killed Kairo, he could play on Delano's emotions, distracting him from trying to take over the Northern cartel.

"AAAAAGHHHHH, NIGGA WHAT THE FUCK DO YOU WANT FROM ME?" Johnny asked as he was feeling the burning sensations drill through his shoulder blade one after another. Delano didn't want shit Johnny had to offer. He wasn't as blood thirsty or money hungry as Johnny. He wanted to put an end to the bullshit that Johnny was keeping up in the streets. He was gone die one painful, slow death, because Delano was going to torture him first.

"Who else could have ordered the attack on my club? If you have control over Detroit, tell me who else could have made that move?" Delano asked, drilling another hole into Johnny's shoulder. He cried out more, refusing to answer Delano each time he asked. Blood was leaking out the holes Delano drilled into Johnny's body.

Finally, Delano got bored of drilling Johnny's skin and wanted to do something more excruciating to break Johnny, so he had Jimenez bring him some pliers. "Now I'm going to ask you again! Each lie you tell me, I'm going take your finger, your toe or tooth, your choice." Delano's threat didn't faze Johnny, he spit right in Delano's face after he gave him his options of torture.

"Bitch, you weak!! My men will be here shortly, so if you gone kill me, you better kill me now, 'cause if I ever get loose I'm gone come for everyone you love, starting with your son then Kairo," Johnny threatened Delano, but he didn't take threats lightly.

"Try me nigga," Delano said, firing a shot into Johnny's left leg missing a main artery. He screamed in pain, he wasn't expecting Delano to torture him like this. If he would have known, he would have never come out of hiding.

"I don't take threats lightly, so watch what the fuck you say to me."

Delano straightened up his fitted white tee that was now covered in Johnny's blood.

"Oh, hell no, get me a doctor!" Johnny demanded, clenching his jaw as he felt every single pain jolt through his body while he sat there helpless, bound to a chair. He scanned the room looking for the weakest link that could aid his escape and came across Jimenez. A soft ass, ruddy nigga, Johnny could smell the weakness off his tatts from across the room. He knew he would flip on Delano in a heartbeat. As Delano turned to walk away to clean himself, Johnny called out to him. "Wait a minute, you're just letting me bleed to death?"

"Jimenez, put 14 grams of cocaine into his wounds," Delano said. He knew cocaine would kill any infections that would manifest, but he wasn't certain what else the drug would do. Meanwhile, Delano headed to his office to shower and change clothes, while Jimenez attended to Johnny's wounds.

"Aghhhh!!!" Johnny yelped in pain as Jimenez patched him up. "Tell me how much he is paying you." Jimenez was hesitant to answer Johnny because he knew his loyalty was with Delano. "Don't be hesitant, tell me so I can triple what he is giving you and give you Southwest Detroit."

"Nah, I'm straight. I don't do deals with the devil," Jimenez responded, wiping down Johnny's blood that was now leaking down the chair. Jimenez was just an attorney, not a thug.

"But you'd rather work for the devil? Because this you're doing is the devil's work," Johnny said, playing on Jimenez's conscience.

"What, and you're not the devil yourself?" Jimenez barked.

"Listen, if you help me escape, I will throw in 75 g's plus give you Southwest Detroit, and you will have my full protection," Johnny offered a deal Jimenez couldn't refuse. He agreed to help Johnny escape, but he needed his money up front. He didn't trust Johnny well enough to go off his word. He witnessed too many sour deals he made with Delano.

NOW DELANO WAS clean from all Johnny's blood, fresh out the shower, stepping off the elevator. He was proud of his accomplishments and wanted to retire from the street life soon. He was tired of moving weight around the country. Once he killed Johnny, he could rest and enjoy his business. Until then, Delano had to go with the flow of things.

He sat down at the bar as his bartender poured him a shot of Hennessey. Meek Mill's "Amen" played through the speakers as Cali came strutting herself into the club right on cue. She was no longer pregnant because she miscarried from the drug abuse. So, she wore a red, shiny, sequin, strapless dress, red Valentino pumps she had stolen from Kairo a while ago and her blonde hair was straightened. She looked like she was a Vegas show girl. She cleaned herself up to make herself look appealing.

"What's up California, what can I do for you?" Delano asked, drinking his shot of Hennessey.

"We need to talk," she demanded, putting five stacks of hundreds on the counter. Delano grabbed Cali by the arm leading her away. He wanted to see what Cali had to say, so he took her to a private room that was closed off from the rest of the club.

"You know better than to drop huge amounts of money like that in front of everyone," Delano scolded, handing Cali 15 pounds of cocaine. She was indeed working for him, playing both sides of the fence though.

"I'm sorry daddy, I'm hoping you can forgive me," Cali begged seductively while getting on her knees unzipping Delano's pants. She took Delano's eight inches out, jerking his dick upward as she licked gently around his balls. Even though Cali was HIV positive, she didn't care if she risked spreading it.

"SHIT! Cali, I thought you said you wanted to talk." Delano shuddered as Cali sucked on his dick gently before gradually increasing her speed. There were no rules to this shit. She knew what she was doing as she looked in Delano's eyes, sucking the life through his penis. Her head wasn't topping Kairo's, but it was enough to get him off. Delano leaned back in the chair as Cali continued to please him.

POW POW POW!!!

Gunshots and screams filled the club, breaking Delano out of his trance. He pushed Cali off him grabbing his AK-47 from under his desk. Cali scooted back smiling, wiping her saliva off the corners of her mouth. Her plan did work, she distracted Delano while Johnny's men came to rescue him.

"Don't you tell Kairo shit, it will kill her!" Delano rushed up front and began to open fire back on Johnny's men.

People were screaming and still running around trying to take cover while Johnny's men attacked, opening fire killing a few of his men on sight. "ESTABAN BAJO ATAQUE A CUBIERTO (*we're under attack, take cover*)!!" Delano yelled, warning the Colombians as they began to fire back. It was hard to see because of the gunsmoke, but the Colombians took out more than half of Johnny's men that day.

The Black Stallion was now a fucking battle ground, a slaughterhouse. Many innocent people that were just visiting the club for the first time were killed. Blood was splattered and feathers from the cushions of the booths were flying around.

"AAAHHHHHH!!!" Mendoza screamed in pain, holding his stomach that was leaking blood. Delano got up and ran over to him immediately. No matter how much Delano applied pressure to his wounds, the bleeding just got worse. Apparently, it was a fatal shot.

"Julio! Julio!!!!" Delano yelled, catching the attention of the other men gathering around them to witness Julio Mendoza's death.

"No, quiero morir, lo siento (*I don't want to die, I'm sorry*)!" he said before choking on his blood and dying. Julio Mendoza suffered from two gunshots to his stomach causing him to bleed to death. He was one of Delano's trusted men and he had to personally deliver the bad news to his wife and children. Delano couldn't just let his death go unnoticed. He held him in his hands watching the blood spill into the carpet. This was the second time Johnny's men attacked Delano's club.

"Boss, we have another problem," Jimenez said as he came into the room rushing towards Delano. He looked up at Jimenez as he held Mendoza in his arms. He didn't want to hear anything else, he didn't give a fuck what happened. He'd just lost one of his best men.

"What is it Jimenez? Delano replied nonchalantly.

"Johnny got away, his men held me at gunpoint, and he escaped," Jimenez lied about the gunpoint, but Johnny did escape in a white van handing Jimenez the 75g's as promised.

"Who the fuck let him go?" Delano said before grabbing Jimenez by the collar, pinning him against the wall. "Who the fuck you work for?"

"Man, watch the fuck out. You know I'm loyal to you," Jimenez said, grunting as Delano continued to pin him against the wall. Delano was taking all his anger and frustration out on Jimenez.

"You sure about that?" Delano said as he let Jimenez go, punching him in the eye. He didn't take that lightly and he swung back and missed. Delano pulled his gun out on Jimenez and aimed it at his head as Jimenez walked up allowing the gun to touch his forehead. Cali walked over the dead bodies, slowly taking the gun out of Delano's hand.

"Go home Delano, you need to rest while we clean up the dead bodies," Cali suggested. Delano knew he needed to rest, so he just left the club and headed straight home.

Delano walked up slowly to his front door covered in Mendoza's blood, unaware Kairo's parents and sisters were there. Kairo ran to him before anyone else could notice. She got Delano into the bathroom, removing his shirt and running the hot shower. Delano stood in the shower with his head against the golden wall and let the water wash the blood down the drain.

"Baby, it's going to be alright!" Kairo said, joining him in the shower. She had no clue what just happened. She still had on her clothes, but she didn't give a damn about getting wet.

"I'm sorry baby, I must have fucked up somewhere," Delano admitted, still feeling guilty about not telling her the truth about Johnny. He had a reason to keep the truth away from Kairo, only to protect her. In this life he'd rather keep her safe and not be sorry.

"Maybe we should postpone the engagement dinner, you need to rest," Kairo suggested, massaging his shoulders. She really looked forward to having this dinner, but her man was more important. He was the king to her world. What's a dinner without her king by her side?

"Baby no, are you sure?" Delano asked. He didn't want her to cancel on her folks because of him. Kairo nodded yes and changed into her robe before going downstairs to dismiss the party. In a way, he was relieved because he really wasn't in the mood to party after what happened earlier. Delano laid back in the bed, thinking about getting revenge on Johnny. He was sick of this nigga was getting off on him like this. Delano knew he had to strike sooner or later.

Fifteen minutes later Kairo came into the room pressing her naked body against Delano's. His dick got hard feeling her warm body press up against his. He couldn't help climbing on top and fucking her, entering her so abruptly, skipping foreplay. He took all his frustrations out on her dry, tight pussy.

"Ouch! Damn Delano, I'm not wet," Kairo moaned in pain, jumping up from underneath him. He didn't realize how hard he was pounding her until she started bleeding. Delano didn't even finish, he just pulled out and went over to the mini bar to make a drink of Dulce.

"Baby, are you sure you're ok?" Kairo slipped back on her robe and followed Delano onto their bedroom patio. She leaned up against his back watching the moonlight shine down onto the waters below. Delano took a sip of his drink before pitching the whole glass into the yard. "Whoa, what the fuck is that about?"

Delano ignored Kairo and walked back into the room, making him another drink. Kairo was confused about Delano's erratic demeanor. He took the whole bottle to the head, gulping it down like water. "You don't hear me talking to you?" Kairo hissed again.

"We found Johnny, and his men shot up my club today looking for him and killed Mendoza." Delano took another gulp, spilling the liquor out the sides of his mouth and wiping it with his hand. "Then California came into the club shortly after you, demanding I give her cocaine."

"Wait a fucking minute." Kairo walked around in disbelief with her hands shaking. "What the fuck you and Cali got going on that I don't know about?" It was time she asked, because ever since that night at the club she'd been meaning to ask.

"No, nothing is going on between California and me. She's a damn crackhead feen, that's all. Come on baby, you know that's all I serve," Delano lied.

Delano didn't want to tell Kairo the truth, because he knew it was going to kill her. They had a lot of disagreements, but no relationship was made perfect. Whenever she was upset or angry with him, she would give him the silent treatment. She got up and returned to bed without even saying goodnight.

"Fuck this!" he yelled, throwing the entire glass bottle of Hennessey into the wall.

"SHH! You're going to wake Chase!" Kairo hissed, walking away to go back to bed. She was livid that Delano was keeping secrets again. He was constantly lying, acting out, and drinking more than usual. Kairo thought it was the wars between the two cartels causing this erratic behavior, when it was really him stepping out on her with Cali.

7

UNDEFEATED

Τhe next morning, Kairo awoke with a wet pussy and an empty side of the bed. *Where the fuck did he go?* she thought to herself. She was horny and normally she and Delano would be making love at this time, it was just their routine. Last night they had a physical argument, but he knew not to lie to her. If she didn't lie to him, why the fuck would he lie to her? She felt like something had changed about him ever since they came back from New Orleans. She just couldn't pinpoint exactly what it was.

She reached into her nightstand pulling out her pink jack rabbit 5000. Taking care of her burning desire to be pleased, she closed her eyes imagining Delano eating her pussy as she made circular motions with her fingers on her clit. Increasing speed with her fingers, she moaned loudly, unaware Jimenez was at the door watching her. His dick began to get hard watching Kairo play with her pussy. Jimenez actually got a thrill out of seeing Kairo naked. He fantasized about what she felt like all the time, so he would get off to the images of her in his mind.

Kairo squeezed her nipples licking them one by one, using her fingers to increase the pleasure. Her body was shaking as she was coming to an orgasm. She tilted her head back rolling her eyes as she came. It was such a strong orgasm that she could feel her heart beating in her clit.

"Mmm, mmm, mmm," Jimenez cleared his throat, walking into the room without knocking, catching Kairo by surprise because she was still naked from masturbating.

"Damn, do you ever knock?" Kairo snapped at him, because this was not the first time he'd walked in on her naked. He'd actually walked in on her twice before without knocking. She knew Jimenez was loyal to Delano, so she didn't think anything odd of it.

"I apologize Kairo, but your mother is here and requesting to see you," he said, pretending not to be staring at her naked body.

"Tell her I will be right down." Kairo threw on her silk robe and rushed down the stairs.

Her mother was sitting in the family room smelling the fresh pink orchids Kairo picked up for the engagement party last night. She spotted Kairo and immediately rushed over to give her a hug. She just saw her last night so she don't know why she was acting like this.

"How is my favorite daughter?" Kairo's mother asked, looking at her while holding Kairo's shoulders. Kairo rolled her eyes, snatching from her mother's grip.

"Mom, I'm fine, you just were here last night!" Kairo replied nonchalantly, walking into the kitchen to pour herself a glass of orange juice. Chase came rushing and running down the stairs jumping into Kairo's arms because he heard her voice.

"Good morning stepmommy!" Chase said, hugging Kairo around the waist as she poured him some orange juice. Although Kairo and Delano weren't yet married, Chase still called Kairo mommy because she was there for him more than Nikki ever was.

"Well who is this little fella?" Kairo's mother asked, surprised, putting her hands on her hips. She was not used to seeing her daughter interact with small children. So, this took her by surprise to see a little child cling onto Kairo like this.

"This is Chase, Momma, Delano's son," Kairo introduced Chase to her mother. He was smiling showing off his teeth as he twisted side to side in the kitchen chairs.

"Oh, ok, well it's nice to meet you Chase." Kairo's mother extended her hand to shake with him. "Kairo, I tell you what, since your father is paying for everything, I need you to go get dressed to go shopping before he changes his mind, while Chase and I sit here and chat," Kairo's mother said excitedly.

Kairo ran upstairs quickly took a hoe bath and got dressed. She wasted no time getting back downstairs to her mom. She asked Rose to keep an eye out for Chase while she spent time with her mother.

"You ready to go wedding dress shopping?" Kairo's mother asked, grabbing her coat and purse.

"Ready as I will ever be." Kairo turned the doorknob letting her mother walk out the door first so she could lock up. As soon as her mother was walking out into the foyer, she stumbled, taking two steps back. "Mom!" Kairo called but got no response and she collapsed onto the floor with a single bullet hole to her head. Blood was gushing from the gun wound down her mother's face. "MOM!!!!!!!!" Kairo screamed again, staring at her dead mother's corpse in the front of her door. "Jimenez!!!" Kairo cried out his name but he was nowhere to be found. Johnny, who was in the kitchen, walked into the common room with a scared Chase in tow.

"No need to be calling for anyone at this moment, they are all dead," Johnny said, coming closer to Kairo as he pointed the silencer at her head. She didn't even realize the blood on the bottom of Johnny's shoes was from Rose's body as she laid there face down in her own blood. Chase was kicking wildly and screaming with his arms stretched towards Kairo. He was terrified. "AYE, SHUT THE FUCK UP!" Johnny yelled at Chase before shooting him in the head.

"NOOOOOOOOOOOOOOOO!!!!!!! WHYYYYYYYYYY!" Kairo screamed as tears rolled down her face. She couldn't believe Johnny would kill an innocent four-year-old. This made Kairo upset. She'd just witnessed her mother and step-son's deaths in cold blood. "WHO THE FUCK ARE YOU, YOU SADISTIC MOTHERFUCKER?!!" Kairo screamed, still standing in the foyer.

"Wow, aren't you a demanding little bitch? I like that," Johnny said as he licked his lips and moved closer with the gun still pointed at Kairo's head.

"You sick son of a b—"

"SHUT THE FUCK UP BITCH!" Johnny slapped Kairo across the face with the silencer, cutting her off. It was that exact moment Kairo realized it was Johnny she was dealing with. She never expected to come face to face with him so soon without having her heat on hand. Johnny's demeanor was more sinister than she thought, killing innocent babies. Kairo got a good glimpse of his bruised eye, looking like he got into a bar fight. She knew he wasn't able to see well out of the one eye, so she thought to attack him in order to get the silencer out his hands.

Before she could even take a leap, someone placed a black bag over her head tying her hands behind her back with rope. She struggled with her abductors, but it seemed as if they were more powerful than her. As they escorted her out the mansion, they forced Kairo to step on her mother's dead body to humiliate her. Kairo was weak, tears ran down her face, and she couldn't believe her mother was killed right in front of her, let alone Delano's son who was in her care. She took all her strength to break free but it didn't work because they had her double tied with a lock to making it impossible for her to escape. They put Kairo in the backseat and purposely hit her head on the hood of the car.

"If you don't stop struggling you will never make it out alive," a woman with a familiar voice said as Kairo got in. "You can remove her bag. I want this bitch to see my face," the woman demanded. Kairo's eyes widened once they removed her bag. It was Cali, her best friend, so she thought. She crossed her smooth legs and waved. "Hi, bitch!"

"What the fuck Cali!!" Kairo yelled. She knew Johnny and Cali were behind her mother getting killed. Kairo resisted, trying to break free to strangle Cali's ass.

"Girl, you can try to get lose all you want, you still gone die," Cali threatened. She hit Kairo in the face with the end of a rifle causing her nose to dislocate and bleed onto her clothes.

"OUCHHH, you broke my nose, you bitch!" Kairo yelled at Cali.

She was now feeling dizzy and lightheaded as the pain of her broken nose moved throughout her entire face.

"Well that's unfortunate, lights out bitch!" Cali said before knocking Kairo out cold for the remainder of the ride.

SPLASH!!!! Kairo's abductors threw a bucket of ice-cold water on her face waking her up from being unconscious. Kairo tried to scream but her mouth was occupied by a mouth gag. She looked around and noticed she was alone in a dark room, tied to a chair over a big pool. The only thing visible was the light shining down on her over the pool. Kairo didn't know how long she'd been out for. All she knew was she was in some trouble and Delano didn't have a clue where she was. He couldn't be there to save her, so Kairo had to save herself.

"Kairo, you don't know who I am, but I'm the man you don't want to piss off." Johnny had a cigar in his hand. His eyes were black as coal, and his voice was so raspy like he smoked cigars all his life. It was just discomforting to hear him speak. "You look even prettier in person than the photos I have of you." He was now touching Kairo's wet face with his rough hands before removing the mouth gag.

"What is it that you want?" she asked, because she didn't have shit to do with Delano and his plans.

"I'm sure you know where Delano is. I want to kill both of you together!" he yelled, kicking her in the knees, pulling out a taser for intimidation. Johnny was going to inflict as much pain on Kairo as Delano did him.

"I have no fucking clue where Delano is. That's your fucking problem to find him, not mine!" Kairo snapped, irritated. Johnny didn't like Kairo's response, so he shocked her in her neck.

"You expect me to believe that? WATCH YO' FUCKING TONE WITH ME BITCH!!!!" He slapped her, and blood spewed from her dislocated nose again. He was in Kairo's face trying to force her to talk. She knew nothing, and even if she did, she was not gone snitch on her man to the enemy. They messed with the wrong bitch.

"Go fuck yourself!" Kairo said, spitting the blood from her nose into his face, the most disrespectful thing she could have ever done in her entire life. This provoked him to point the gun at her temple, ready to squeeze the trigger at any moment.

"Johnny, don't you do nothing you will regret. We need her alive!" Cali said, walking out of the darkness and slowly taking the gun away from him.

He left the room before he killed Kairo off impulse, because that's what he was going to do if she said another word. He had that trigger-happy hand, killing anyone he saw fit to kill, just because he could. Kairo sat there tied to a chair, bound by chains and rope, overwhelmed about all that was taking place. She couldn't believe she trusted this bitch. She had the nerve to betray her, after all she had done for her. Kairo was the strings to the fiddle and Cali just played her until she couldn't anymore.

"Hey, you not so tough now, are you?" Cali tormented as she strutted her way over to Kairo wearing gold six-inch heels and a tight leather dress.

"You're one backstabbing ass bitch. I'm whooping your ass when I get loose!" Kairo said, meaning every word that came out of her mouth. She sat there contemplating how she was gone catch this bitch slipping.

"Ha! Kairo, when are you gone realize I'm not scared of you? You took my life away from me, from my son, my other kids," Cali nagged on and on about the past and how Kairo ruined it by coming into Delano's life.

"What the fuck, what you are talking about?? It doesn't matter because I'm whooping your ass when I get free," Kairo threatened again. She didn't give a fuck what Cali was talking about. Kairo was gone beat her ass once she got loose. Cali laughed, grabbing Kairo's hair and tightening it around her fist. Her head was already hurting from earlier when they purposely hit her head on the car's hood. Then Cali took a pair of scissors, cutting off Kairo's long hair.

"Bitch, why are you doing this?" Kairo asked as Cali continued to snip her hair off piece by piece.

"Aht, aht, hoe, that's not the way to talk to a friend," Cali retorted, now taking the clippers and shaving Kairo's hair completely bald. This was by far the most fun Cali had, besides her killing Don and Mr. Banks. Cali had Don's body chopped up limb by limb and disposed into the Detroit River, since he wanted to be gay and give her HIV.

"Please Cali, why are you doing this to me?" Kairo's voice was now weak from her crying, but she was far from weak. This bitch knew how to survive even in the coldest winter. It was just the principle. She'd been her friend all this time and now she wanted to be her enemy.

"You are weak, and you're going to be tortured and killed just like you were supposed to be from the beginning." Cali shaved Kairo's hair off completely, leaving her with a Lil' Boosie fade.

"Bravo, bravo, big sis with the clippers. I might need you to shave me up next," Johnny said as he was clapping his hands and entering the room. Kairo realized her own friend she'd known for quite some time now was working with the enemy, deceiving her. Not only was she deceitful, but she was a backstabbing, manipulative cunt.

"It was me who killed your mother. I shot the bitch right in her skull from the car, and also it was me who killed Mr. Banks, trying to give you the death sentence. All so I could have my life back with Delano," Cali spat into Kairo's ears. She had never seen this side from Cali before, maybe the drugs were just a cover up.

"Bitch, you're sick." Kairo spit in Cali's face, the most disrespectful thing Kairo could have ever done. Cali wasn't even expecting that. She took her fingers to clear away the spit and pulled the lever releasing Kairo into the pool down below. Cali and Johnny watched as Kairo murmured, twisting and turning in the water, finally bringing her up for air. Kairo was choking and gasping for air. She'd never been more afraid to lose her life as much as today.

"You are even more pathetic than I thought," Cali said, breathing in Kairo's face with her hot ass breath. The only reason Cali was even saying what she was saying was because she had niggas in the next room that would jump on Johnny's order if he said jump. Other than that, Kairo would have no problem whooping her ass. "You want to tell me where Delano is?" Cali asked, but Kairo just sat there ignoring her as she thought of ways to escape.

"Ok, let's play a game. It's called pin the tail on the donkey," Johnny suggested, calling his men into the room, which in this case Kairo was the donkey. He then ordered two women dressed in Playboy bunny outfits to come and remove Kairo out her chains and strip her down naked.

"Wait, what the fuck is you do—mmmm, mmmm," Kairo was asking before they covered her mouth with the gag ball, muffling out her words. They continued to strip her completely naked in front of everyone.

"You had a chance to speak and you still refused to talk, so now maybe this will help." Johnny walked around crossing his arms. The women laid Kairo stretched out on the wooden table, using the same chains to bind her with. Kairo had no clue what was about to take place next, so she laid there stretched out with saliva just escaping from her mouth. The ropes and chains were cutting into her skin and if she moved, its clutches would become tighter. This was like some bondage shit off a porno, except it was Kairo getting raped. "Men, do as you please," Johnny ordered. I had to be about 30 men in that room. Some wore a condom and some didn't, and some watched her as they were jerking themselves off to the sight of her being raped.

Tears started to escape from the corner of Kairo's eyes as she could feel her body being violated in the most atrocious way. She couldn't move, she had no choice but to lay there and let these men have their way with her. The whole time she wondered where the fuck was Delano. He said he would protect her all his life, but he wasn't there.

After all the men raped Kairo, they threw her into a small closet with both of her hands and feet still tied together. Her anus was bleeding and throbbing in pain, because she was also violated back there. They were trying to do whatever they could to get Kairo to break so she would snitch and give up Delano's location, but she was no snitch. She would die first before she snitched on Delano or anybody. *I wonder is this how Johnny makes people fear him, if so, he sure has a shitty way of making people surrender*, Kairo thought to herself as she laid there in her own blood. She was cringing and holding onto her stomach while it began to hurt. Kairo was broken in half, but she would never let Cali and Johnny see it.

"Cali, I have to pee, please!" Kairo called out to Cali because she had a plan. It was a risky one, but it was well worth the shot. Cali was talking to the men while Johnny left to go looking for Delano. His plan to take Delano out the game was almost complete.

"Piss on yourself," Cali retorted, walking past the closet.

"Please, I'll—"

"You'll what? If I let you use the bathroom, you better be quick," Cali said, picking Kairo up and taking her to the restroom.

"Well I can't wipe myself if I'm tied up." Kairo was eyeing the same pair of scissors Cali used to cut her hair off with, on Cali's hip.

"Don't try nothing stu—" Kairo elbowed Cali in face, catching her completely off guard. Before Cali could finish warning her, Kairo flipped the ropes around Cali's neck strangling her. Then she locked Cali's hair around her fist just as she did her, and bashed her forehead into the glass mirror. Blood instantly rushed down her face as she tried to fight back. Cali was struggling in her six-inch pumps, losing her balance.

Kairo had an agenda, to kill this bitch without any remorse, but that wasn't enough to send her to her maker, so she took her head bashing it, breaking the sink. This caused the water and blood to spill everywhere. Kairo checked her pulse and she was still alive, just unconscious. She got the fuck on as the bathroom was now filling with Cali's blood and water.

Picking up the scissors, Kairo cut herself free and took the clothes off Cali leaving her in her lace bra and undies. Kairo snuck out the restroom and ran to the other side of the hallway. She needed a gun, so she waited for the opportunity to present itself. Two men were talking in the room, and Kairo waited for the weakest link to get caught slipping so she could take him hostage. One man dressed in jeans and a white tee started walking towards the door.

"Whoa, what the fu—" he stammered as Kairo covered his mouth, wrapping the ropes around his throat.

"Scream and I will snap your fucking neck in two places," Kairo put him in firm chokehold position. Something she learned from her brothers when she was younger. "Give me your gun!" she demanded, pinning one of his arms behind his back.

"Do, you even know how to shoot a gun?" he asked as he was struggling to get free from Kairo's chokehold. She glanced at him wishing he would have just cooperated with her, but now she had to kill this man. Time was precious and Kairo didn't have time for small talk.

"Alright, snapping your neck in two it is then," she huffed.

"Ok I'll—" *CRACKK CRACK!* He tried to say something, but it was too late, she snapped his neck from ear to ear twice. Watching his 240-pound body go THUD! Onto the floor alarming the other men in the room. Kairo took both guns off his hip, when his body dropped, for protection. The other men came out to see what that loud thud was and by the time they reached the hallway, Kairo held both guns in her hands in their face, standing over their partner's dead body.

"Alright, fuck boys, tell me how the fuck I get out of here." Kairo raised the guns aiming it at their heads. She was ready to shoot, but they didn't take her seriously.

"Man, watch out, have you ever shot a gun before?" the younger one of them asked, laughing at her. She aimed the gun at the older man and pulled the trigger. *POW!*

"AAAHHH, GOD DAMN IT!" the older man shouted after she shot him in his right thigh. He was holding his leg that was now bleeding profusely.

"It's funny your friend right here asked me the same thing, and I snapped his neck in two places. Does that answer your question?" She walked closer to the younger man with her gun pointed at his heart. Delano taught her how to shoot to kill, not injure.

"Uh, yea, yea, yea." The young man was stuttering, putting both of his hands up in the air surrendering. He had sweat dripping down his face and might have shit in his pants. She assumed he never had a gun pointed at his heart before.

"You're going to help me get the fuck out of here," Kairo demanded, touching the young man's chest with the barrel of the gun.

"And if I refuse?"

"Really, what's your name son?"

"Roy Allen Jr," he replied, watching Kairo closely.

"Roy, you must have a death wish or something, so here's what's going to happen if you decide to refuse. I'm going to shoot two bullets in your skull and if you're still alive, I'm going to put this gun so far up your ass like y'all did me on that table and shoot inside your intestines. You will die a slow but painful death," Kairo threatened the young man.

"Alright, I don't want no smoke." Roy surrendered and got on board. "What about him?"

"He's about to be dead in the next few minutes." Kairo stuck the barrel of the gun deep in his bullet wound, pushing it further into his blood stream. "Remember me? The same bitch you stuck your dirty dick in," Kairo whispered to him before shooting him in his heart. Soon as Kairo turned around, a bullet ripped through her lower calf. Johnny caught her trying to escape and shot her in her calf so she couldn't run. Shocked from the pain that was protruding in her lower calf, she fell to her knees and fell before Roy Allen Jr.

8

A BLOOD SPREE

Delano hadn't even touched down in Colombia yet before Jimenez called him with the bad news. He was a thousand miles away from home, when he had the pilot turn around immediately, arriving back to Detroit faster than he left. The news sent him over the edge about his son. Chase was only four and knew nothing about what was happening. How was he going to explain to Nikki, once she was released from prison, that their four-year-old son was killed? He had no words to express the anger he felt, all he had on his mind was murder. He was about to go on a blood spree, killing Johnny and whoever else was working for him.

He went straight to his storage unit to get his sniper equipment and met up with Harvey, who was Johnny's current driver, to get Johnny's shipment location. *It's a shame how people betray their leaders for a rock or two,* he thought. He was tired of playing fair, but Johnny had went too fucking far invading his space and killing his son.

He was not expecting Kairo's mother, out of all people, to get killed in their front foyer, nor did he suspect Kairo being kidnapped either. In this drug business you learned not to trust anyone. *How the fuck did Johnny get my location?* Delano thought to himself, because only a few knew, and his new place was undisclosed. You can't even google the address. He had a gut ass feeling someone from his crew was being a traitor, and he had to get to the bottom of it.

He pulled up to Johnny's shipment location meeting up with the Colombians, letting his Uzi rip into everybody in his way. No one was left alive. He raided his whole shipment taking every drug Johnny had, cocaine, heroin, crystal meth, anything that was valuable. Even the new shipment that was flown in from Italy. Since Johnny was fucking with his life, he was gone fuck up his money. Just by Delano tampering with Johnny's shipment, this was about to put Johnny in a whole lot of trouble with the Italians.

He had over 27 gallons of gasoline, and had the Colombians torch that warehouse to the ground with all the dead bodies inside. It wasn't long before Johnny got the message his shipment was stolen, along with 200 workers being dead. He put Kairo in the truck with him and headed over to his warehouse to see what was going on. Johnny didn't know he was headed to his own death trap. His mind was only on one thing and that was him being fucked, 3 million in a whole with the Italians.

Delano had the Colombians spread out throughout the tall grass, laying low as they patiently waited until Johnny and his crew showed up. He set up his sniper rifle equipment, testing the scope and loading his M80 with ammunition. He didn't want to involve violence, but he did what he had to do.

BEEP BEEP! The tracker notification alerted Delano about the incoming vehicle as Johnny's black Escalade approached the gate. Delano peered through his scope so he could get a clear shot of his targets without missing. Johnny's men got out one by one, letting Kairo, who was limping badly, out last. Delano recognized she was shot in her lower calf, and her hair was completely shaved off. Seeing Kairo in this condition inspired him to show Johnny no mercy. Johnny stood in the middle of the dirt path placing a call to the Italians explaining that his warehouse was involved in a drug bust.

Delano clipped the silencer so they couldn't hear where the bullets were coming from and began to let his machine rip into their bodies. Catching them one by one, shooting niggas in their heads, he had them falling and they didn't know which direction the shots were coming from. Kairo began screaming and made Johnny look back, and he noticed his men were dropping like flies. He dropped his phone and stood there with his hands up surrendering. He was weak and absolutely nothing without his men.

"Delano, I know you're around here somewhere. How clever of you to make a move like that!" Johnny said, still surrendering, unaware if Delano was going to kill him or not. Now Johnny knew he was fucked, so he grabbed his pocketknife threatening to slice Kairo's throat. Delano walked up out of the tall grass, wanting to look Johnny in the eyes before he killed him. He wasn't about to do the back and forth thing, he was about to kill him clean off.

"Johnny, what is all this going to prove? I killed the majority of your men, you have no money, and you have no product. You don't have shit to lose. Killing Kairo is only going to land a bullet in your head," Delano said as he slowly approached Johnny.

"I do this shit for my family," he replied.

"Family? Nigga you killed my son today and he was only four. What the fuck you know about family?" Delano kept calm. Even though he was angry about his son's death, he didn't want to risk getting Kairo killed. He kept talking to Johnny, distracting him from Kairo. She waited for Johnny's most vulnerable moment before she jabbed her elbow in his throat causing him to drop the knife.

"Move away Kairo!" Delano yelled, and she moved away immediately. Johnny tried to run but Delano didn't show him any mercy as he emptied his clip in Johnny's body. He let all his frustration out as he squeezed the trigger. *POW!* One for his son Chase. *POW!* Two for Kairo's mother. *POW!* Three for Kairo. After that Delano kept firing shots. *POW POW POW POW!!!* As Johnny's body slowly hit the ground.

"Baby, we got to get the fuck out of here, the police coming!" Kairo said in a panicky voice as she tugged on Delano, breaking him out his trance. He was sure he killed Johnny. After all, he watched his body hit the ground so there was no need for him to check his pulse. They jumped into Delano's truck as the wailing sound of the firetrucks,

95

ambulance and police sirens were nearby. "Baby, I was raped. I need to go to the emergency room!" Kairo busted out in tears.

"Baby, I'm sorry you had to endure that. I promise you I will take care of you," Delano made another promise.

At this point, she wasn't listening to him because he left her when he promised to protect her from the beginning. Delano understood Kairo's pain. He knew he failed to keep her safe, so he just held her hand on the way to Sani Grace Hospital. On the bright side, she was just happy to see Johnny dead, but Cali was the only one she still had to deal with. She was unaware Delano and Cali were still messing around with each other, so she felt the need not to tell him about her.

THE NEXT MORNING, the time was 9:25 am when Kairo awoke to the sunlight beaming through her bedroom window. After leaving the emergency room at four, she was in a lot of pain, feeling a bit drowsy from the pain meds the doctors prescribed. Delano thought it was best to spend the night at her condo, instead of driving all the way back to New Baltimore, Michigan. All her tests came back negative for HIV, chlamydia, and syphilis, but she tested positive for trichinosis and gonorrhea. Kairo never had an STD before, so she wasn't feeling too good. She had a fever and a sore throat along with a bullet wound from being shot by Johnny.

"Hey baby, you hungry?" Delano asked Kairo as he entered the room, pulling the curtains together. She shook her head no and continued to snuggle under the covers. "Jimenez will be here shortly. He will be taking you up north."

"You are leaving me again?" Kairo asked, sitting up in bed. "Do you have any fucking clue as to what I've been through? I lost my mother and got kidnapped because you wanted to leave me!" Kairo yelled.

Delano perfectly understood how Kairo felt, but in these streets, there was no such thing as killing a leader and the clan not retaliating. That's why he called Jimenez. They discussed laying low up north for a while. He knew it was only a matter of time before the Northern cartel came to revenge Johnny's death. He failed the first time, letting his guard down, and Johnny was able to get at Kairo by destroying her pride. He was not willing to risk Kairo's life any more than he already had.

Kairo was not happy to hear that Delano was shipping her off. This was the most critical time she needed him and he was yet abandoning her again. So, Jimenez took Kairo up north and there they stayed for one month.

9

GUILT FREE

1 MONTH LATER

The cold winter was hitting hard, and Kairo watched as Jimenez was outside chopping logs for the fireplace. It was so cold outside you could see the frost sticking to the windows as the snow continued to fall onto the ground. Kairo hated the wintertime, it was her least favorite season of the year. She'd rather it be the summertime so it could be sunny and hot all year long. At least in the summer, you don't have to worry about sliding on ice and risking breaking something.

"Good morning Jimenez, have you heard anything from Delano?" Kairo asked him as soon as he stepped foot into the door, allowing the cool breeze to follow behind him. He shook his head no, stomping both feet onto the mat getting the excess snow off his boots, while removing his gloves. His fingers were frozen together, before using his hot breath to blow onto them. To help with that, she fixed them both a cup of hot cocoa and sat with him in front of the fireplace.

"Hmm, this is so not like Delano to go without seeing me. He must be ashamed of me," Kairo complained out loud so that Jimenez could hear her. This was the longest she and Delano had been away from each other since they'd been back together. He would her call once a week, and this was driving her crazy. She felt it was not fair he was distant as hell for no reason. Although she knew the consequences of dating a street nigga, this was something different for Kairo.

"Kairo, in this drug life it's to be expected to not hear from your significant other, let alone having sex with them. Sex would be the last thing on our minds when we are trying to protect the people we love. If I'm being honest, I don't think he deserves you," Jimenez replied. He was tired of hearing Kairo complain.

"You really don't think so?"

"Hell no, look how he just abandoned you." Jimenez took a sip of his hot cocoa sitting the cup back onto the table. This made Kairo shut down. She knew Delano loved her, she just wasn't sure why he wouldn't talk to her more on a regular basis.

"You know what, you're right. So what can we do about it?" Kairo asked.

"There is nothing we can do but just wait until he further instructs us, but in the meantime, I still can do this." Jimenez leaned in to kiss Kairo on her soft lips. She didn't even stop him, she just continued to kiss him back. "I'm sorry, is this weird?" Jimenez stopped and held onto the back of Kairo's neck, pulling her in closer.

"Yes, but I'm horny as fuck!" Kairo replied, still kissing Jimenez back. One thing led to another, and Kairo removed her shirt exposing her perky breast while Jimenez sucked on them and unfastened his pants revealing his hard dick. He was no Delano, but Kairo was sexually deprived so anything would feel good right now. She straddled Jimenez, riding his face and cumming all over his tongue. If Jimenez's dick was pre-cumming just from tasting her savory pussy juices, just imagine what it would feel like once he entered her.

Jimenez turned Kairo over on her stomach, inserting himself inside her warmness. He liked to fall inside her, Kairo's pussy was too fucking good to him. Jimenez increased his speed, smacking both of her ass cheeks. She threw her hips back in a circular motion as Jimenez pounded her harder. They both were so lost in fucking they didn't hear Delano walk into the cabin. He was standing there for two minutes, shocked to see his fiancée fucking one of his loyal men. Out of all the things he could have seen, he didn't expect to walk in on this.

As Jimenez turned over from sweating and panting from working Kairo, he jumped out of his skin and so did Kairo once she turned around. She was just as shocked as Delano, that she just got caught fucking another man.

"Nah, don't let me stop you, gone ahead continue to fuck her," Delano instructed, but Jimenez refused. "Bitch, I said continue!!" Delano screamed, aiming the gun at Kairo and Jimenez, who was now struck by guilt. Not sure what Delano was going to do, Jimenez continued to fuck Kairo as she began to cry from being caught. "Don't fucking cry now, you are being a hoe!" Delano came around to grab her chin, making her look up at him.

"Please don't do this Delano!" Kairo cried hysterically, as Jimenez kept up his pace.

"Do what, put a fucking bullet in Jimenez's head?" Delano asked before shooting Jimenez directly in his head, causing blood to splatter all over the room.

"NOOOOOOOOOOOOOOOOOOOO!!!!!!" Kairo screamed, crawling into the corner. Her heart was racing as she just witnessed a murder. Delano followed her over to the corner and pointed the gun directly at Kairo's head.

"You really gone make me kill you?" Delano said with one tear escaping from his eye before pulling the trigger, emptying his clip into Kairo's body.

ANNNT ANNTT ANNTTT!! The alarm clock went off waking Kairo from her dream. Her heart was beating frantically and out of control as she wiped the beads of sweat from her forehead. Looking down, she checked her heart and head for bullets, but none were there. She then realized it was just another dream she was having and she'd been experiencing the same dream for almost a week now. Kairo suffered from post-traumatic stress badly. Having flashbacks from the rape, being shot by Johnny, watching Chase get killed and stepping on her dead mother's corpse all factored in her stress. Nonetheless, her leg was getting better day by day. The Voodoo queen sent another magic elixir to help with the healing of her lower calf.

Kairo walked into the bathroom and examined her body before

turning the shower on. One thing was true, she hadn't seen Delano in months. Her body craved for some sexual pleasure, but how could she fulfill her desire if her man was miles away? Kairo stepped inside the steaming hot shower and touched herself in all the arousing areas. She still wasn't happy with fingering herself; she wanted much more than that. Finally having enough of fantasizing, Kairo got out, dried her skin and got dressed.

"Fuck this, I need some dick right now," Kairo mumbled out loud, unaware Jimenez overheard her and he was going to use that to his advantage. She then came out the room in her robe looking for Jimenez and found him in the kitchen. He hurried over to the fridge, pretending to be looking for something to drink, and pulled out a carton of Egg Nog.

"Good morning, Kairo," Jimenez spoke as he poured himself a glass of Egg Nog.

"Hey, good morning, I need the keys. I want to go to the city today," Kairo demanded, holding her hand out. He looked at her and hesitated before responding back to her.

"You know I can't let you go to the city," Jimenez said, walking over to the table to sit down.

"Why can't I go to the city? I feel like a fucking prisoner. I hate it here!!!" Kairo screamed, stomping back to the room. Kairo wasn't about to let Jimenez stop her from going to the city. Even if she had to wait to steal the car while he was sleep, so be it. Jimenez knocked on Kairo's door to make sure she was fully dressed before entering.

"Kairo, I am simply protecting you. Delano doesn't want you anywhere near Detroit," Jimenez warned Kairo, while standing in the doorway to her room.

"Jimenez, I know you did not just come in here to tell me no shit like that when I am more than capable of defending myself," Kairo said, offended, jumping up from the bed, pushing Jimenez out the room. Jimenez grabbed Kairo and kissed her, finally getting to do what he had been dreaming to do.

"What the fuck Jimenez!" Kairo shouted, wiping the kiss off her lips. She was shocked he would even make such a bold move. Kairo backed up because this reminded her of her dream she'd been having.

"I'm sorry Kairo, I just fell in love with you and I—" Kairo slapped Jimenez before he could finish explaining himself.

"Do you want to fucking die?" Kairo asked him. He was still shocked he just got slapped and nodded no.

"Don't you ever say no stupid shit like that ever again!" Kairo slammed the door in his face. She was scared, the dream she was having was coming true. She didn't want to lose her life, nor did she want Jimenez to die.

Kairo was determined to go back to the city, so she looked in her dresser and pulled out her 9mm. and loaded it with the bullets. Nobody was going to stop her from living her life, so she went into the living room and pointed the gun at Jimenez, demanding he turn over the keys. At first Jimenez refused until she fired a shot into the TV.

"Damn woman, what the fuck am I supposed to watch now? You done shot the TV," Jimenez said, handing her the keys.

"I don't know, but I got to get the fuck out of here." Kairo left out to go start the car. Only problem was, the car wouldn't start because the battery was dead. Kairo screamed, hitting her hands on the freezing cold steering wheel. She was in the north in the middle of nowhere with no dick or sanity. Jimenez made a phone call before he looked outside and saw Kairo crying inside the car.

"Come on Kairo, it's cold out here!" Jimenez yelled from the porch of the cabin house.

Kairo took the keys out the ignition. "Alright! Give me just one damn minute!" she yelled and walked back into the house. Her face was facing the floor because she was embarrassed.

"You don't have to be ashamed. Look, I'm here, I have always been here." Jimenez took Kairo into his arms and hugged her tightly. He really had strong feelings towards Kairo, and he wanted to express how he felt. "Kairo, I have always been there for you, except that one time, but I'm here with you now."

"You know Delano wouldn't like that. Don't overstep your boundaries," Kairo warned Jimenez.

Jimenez pulled Kairo in for a sloppy kiss. "Fuck boundaries, I want you," Jimenez admitted. He did want Kairo ever since he met her. It wasn't like Jimenez wasn't attractive. He was indeed a very handsome Colombian, although he was short at 5'7, and he had tattoos all over his body. She just didn't date outside her race.

Kairo couldn't help but to kiss Jimenez because her hormones was all over the place; plus, he was the only one around. Delano no longer mattered to her, as she began to remove her clothes one by one, making a trail from the living room to the bedroom as Jimenez followed. There were cameras in every room that Delano installed just in case someone found out Kairo's location. Jimenez knew about it because he stumbled across them changing a blown lightbulb in his room. He suspected Delano to not trust him after a while, but Delano never let it be known.

This was all part of Jimenez's set up, to lure Delano to the cabin and avenge Johnny's death by using Kairo, because he knew she was going to be gullible and fall for his smooth talk. After all, Jimenez was an educated lawyer. He knew how to manipulate in order to get what he wanted.

"You got a condom?" Kairo asked, and Jimenez pulled one from his back pocket, because he was already prepared for what was about to come next. Jimenez was already on hard from all the times he fantasized about her soft body, and he was now about to get ready to finally experience it.

Jimenez tore the golden wrapper and inserted his average-size penis inside Kairo's warmness. She was now cured and cleared up from all her STDs, so sex was normal to have again. Jimenez didn't last very long, and this made Kairo upset.

"What a waste of dick," Kairo said to herself as she laid on Jimenez's chest falling asleep. She had no clue Delano knew about the betrayal from watching them on the cameras, because she didn't know they existed. While she lay asleep, Jimenez made his move and called Johnny's crew, giving them the location of the cabin house.

Delano came in waking them up, catching them in the bed together. Kairo ran to the corner, suddenly remembering the dream.

"Kairo, get dressed. Let's go for a ride," Delano suggested, but Kairo refused out of fear that he might kill her. "Kairo, I'm not going to ask you again, get dressed now!" Delano yelled at her as if she was a child. This time Kairo got up and got dressed without missing a beat. Changing his mind about the ride, Delano ordered her to stay.

"Delano, why are you doing this?" Kairo asked as tears fell down her face.

"Don't ask questions now, after you've been caught. You weren't crying when he had his penis in your guts. That's where mine belongs, you belong to me," Delano said, grabbing a chair and sitting down. Delano was uneasy about this situation. He waved the gun back and forth. His best man for years and the love of his life were sleeping together.

"Delano, please—" Jimenez opened his mouth to speak, but Delano jumped up and pointed the gun at his mouth.

"I TRUSTED YOU!" Delano yelled as tears rolled down his face. Delano was a strong man; he hadn't cried since his father and Chase died. Delano thought Jimenez and he were tighter than that. "Why did you do this?" Delano asked Jimenez.

"Because someone had to be here for her. You don't deserve her anyway."

"Oh, but you do?" Delano stepped up in Jimenez's face. Unmindful Jimenez was going to punch Delano in the face causing things to escalate quickly.

"STOPPPPPP IT!!!!" Kairo screamed as both men were now tearing each other's flesh apart. Delano's nose began to leak blood as Jimenez gave him an upper cut. Kairo was freaking out, she grew up with her brothers fighting and she didn't like that. So she ran to pick up the gun Delano dropped before firing two shots into the ceiling. Delano and Jimenez both stopped fighting as Kairo turned the gun on them.

"What the fuck Kairo!" Delano said, getting up to take the gun out of Kairo's hand.

"Not so fucking fast, but do you hear that?" Kairo said, walking over to the window still pointing the gun towards Delano. To her surprise, they were surrounded by Johnny's crew. "Delano, we have a fucking problem!" Kairo was starting to panic.

"Man, what?" Delano rushed over to the window. "Oh shit, we need to get the fuck out of here." Delano looked up at Jimenez, suddenly realizing no one knew of their location because Jimenez was the only one he gave it to. Kairo didn't even know the city she was in so it couldn't be her. The only person that knew of their location was Jimenez.

"Jimenez, you did this. How much is he paying you?" Delano looked him straight in the eyes demanding an answer. He wanted to know why he would switch now after all these years, when his grand-father raised them both together. Jimenez just stood there with his nose turned up. He wasn't going to tell him what Johnny had given him.

He didn't even have to respond. Delano noticed the tattoo while they were fighting. His heart was shattered someone he used to call his brother would be betray him twice. Delano got the gun from Kairo and didn't hesitate to shoot Jimenez in both of his eyes. *POW POW POW!* Shots rang through the house as they fell onto the floor to avoid the bullets and the shards of glass that were flying everywhere. Delano built a tunnel to escape and grabbed Kairo as they ran quickly.

"When we get home, we need to talk," Delano said to Kairo while opening the hatch to the tunnel. He was smart to engineer an underground tunnel that would take him to the city just in case shit like this ever happened. Once underground, Delano hit a red flashing button signaling the cabin to blow up. Everything and everyone that was within 60 feet was blown into tiny pieces. Dust and debris from the explosion above them rained down on them causing them to cough. They walked for three miles without saying a single word to each other.

"Delano, you have—" Kairo started to speak, but Delano wasn't hearing it.

"Shut up Kairo, don't talk to me." Delano kept walking, but Kairo wasn't about to go for that. She wanted her chance to explain.

"No, fuck you, you're going to listen to me!" Kairo screamed, pushing Delano in his back. He reacted by slapping her across the face. Kairo gasped, holding her cheek because Delano had never hit her before. He didn't even apologize, he just kept walking until a tunnel vehicle picked them up. Kairo kept her distance, trying to make sure she didn't get slapped again. She did this all the way until they reached their destination, New Baltimore, dropping them off right underneath the mansion.

"Why the fuck would you do me like that?" Delano asked as they climbed up and walked into their home.

"Do you really want to go there?" Kairo responded, putting her hands on her hips. She was just too done with this man. He slapped her without even apologizing. "Why do you think it's ok to leave me for months at a time, then get mad at me for getting some dick?" Kairo hissed, rolling her eyes.

"I apologize for hitting you, but this is what you need to understand. You are my woman, you can't carry my last name in these streets if you gone be fucking my men behind my back. You look like you're loose and ran through. If I wasn't in love with you then I would have put three bullets in your skull," Delano said to Kairo in an irritated tone. He really was hurting on the inside. The woman he loved just turned her back on him.

"But you know what happened to me!" She really felt like he should understand.

"Kairo, I understand those men hurt you, but you also hurt me—"

"NO, YOU DON'T!!! YOU DON'T KNOW WHAT THEY DID TO ME!!" Kairo yelled, cutting Delano off. She burst into tears, because the very next day after she told him about the rape, Delano shipped her up north with Jimenez. You would think he would have been there for her, but Delano was a street nigga. His mind was programmed on killing Johnny, and that's exactly what he did, he killed him. Nothing else mattered to him at the time. Now, Kairo felt like Delano abandoned her and was no longer in love with her, but that wasn't the case at all.

"Baby, stop crying," Delano said, consoling Kairo in the middle of their living room as the moonlight beamed directly on them. He really was hurt too. He lost his four-year-old son and two of his best men as well, but he still found it in his heart to forgive Kairo. Otherwise, he would have killed her immediately just from her committing the act of cheating on him, but Delano also cheated on Kairo, so karma was paying him back. Delano hated to see Kairo cry, it made him weak on the inside. He knew he was wrong for leaving Kairo in Jimenez's arms.

"Baby, in these streets, one thing you need to always remember. Long as you are alive you will always be a target for my downfall. It's better to get than to get got," Delano said, holding Kairo close while kissing her on the forehead. They both cried together, holding each other because they both had been through a lot these past couple of months. No matter what they'd been through, they always bounced back stronger than before. After they cried together, they made love and fell asleep holding each other.

10

ALL SHIT ROLLS DOWN THE HILL

C ali took her last inhale of what was left of her cigarette and flickered it into the trash can. Everyone thought she was dead because she disappeared, but she was rescued. Once Johnny saw the blood and water spilling from the bathroom into the hallway, he immediately called an ambulance to get her the medical attention she needed.

They arrived within 15 minutes of receiving the call and were able to revive Cali, rushing her to Receiving Hospital. She spent two weeks in the intensive care unit, receiving two blood transfusions for losing a significant amount of blood, and two weeks in the recovery unit.

Although Cali had to get surgery and two blood transfusions, she still remembered everything as if it happened yesterday. She looked at herself in the mirror and saw the scars from Kairo bashing her head into the mirror and on the sink, and was ready to go kill her. "AAAG-GHHHHH!" Cali screamed, taking her fist and breaking the mirror. She no longer was the same, she was now ugly and resembled the Chucky doll.

From that point on, Cali had set a personal vendetta against Kairo. Whenever she saw her again, she was going to kill her on site. She felt like Kairo ruined her life. She caused Cali's face to be badly disfigured with scars all over.

With her being hospitalized, it was a whole month Cali was without drugs. The doctors played a significant role, warning her that if she continued to use those drugs, she was only speeding up the process of dying because she already had HIV. This was the most sober Cali had ever been in her entire life. She was stronger than ever, gained a little weight and might have steered away from drugs for good. She wanted to change her life, maybe work on getting her kids back, but she didn't have a home to give them.

She stepped outside, allowing the cool air to fall fresh onto her skin as she waited patiently for her ride. The sunlight reflected off the snow, making it impossible for her to see, so she went back in and waited in the hallway. She was dying on the inside for another cigarette, but let any drug counselor tell it, cigarettes were considered a trigger to relapse into her old drug habits. She was not looking to go back down that path.

So, she looked in her purse and came across some old, stale ass Double Mint gum. This would just have to do for now. She wasn't about to fuck up her one-month sobriety for anybody. Cali went through too much to fall flat onto her face again. All the countless and sleepless nights, having withdrawals, she lost more than she gained.

Today was the day she was able to start over fresh and breathe again regardless of what she'd been through. Being HIV positive and addicted to drugs was not the best highlights of her life. She had a miscarriage because of the stress weighing on her body. There was no doubt in her mind that if she went full term, the state would have taken that baby just like they took the last four. Cali realized her cell phone died and her ride had not pulled up yet. *Man, where the fuck are these people at?* Cali thought to herself before she picked up a nearby pay phone to dial Delano.

This whole time she was laid in a hospital bed, clinging onto her life from what occurred between her and Kairo, she knew she would have to be prepared to tell Delano why she went MIA. She knew he tried to contact her to do some runs.

"Hello," Delano answered within the third ring.

"Hey, this is Ca-Cali, are you busy?" she stuttered, gripping the pay phone, afraid Kairo might have told Delano about her involvement. Little did she know, Kairo didn't because she didn't have the chance to tell him.

"Man, where you been? You disappeared and I need my shit delivered on time," Delano spoke plainly.

"I know, I been in the hospital. You think you can come get me?" Cali asked.

"Hospital?" Delano questioned. That was one place he was not expecting her to be.

"Yea, can you come get me? I'm at Receiving," she asked again.

"Alright," Delano said before ending the call.

Just as discussed, Delano pulled up within forty-five minutes. He was already in the city, dropping Kairo off at her people's house. Cali saw him and rushed to get inside his truck, forgetting her face was badly disfigured. He gave Cali that look, as he silently wondered what the fuck happened to her. She caught a glimpse of him staring at her from her side view and decided to speak.

"I know, I look horrible, but can you stop staring at me?" Cali hissed. Plugging her phone up, she was now feeling insecure about her scars. She'd never felt so embarrassed than she was now, even though he had known her since she was 14.

Delano put his hands up. "My bad, I just was wondering what happened to you. Do you know where you're trying to go?"

"No, I don't have anywhere to go. I was staying in a women's shelter, but since I've been gone an entire month, I'm sure my spot is gone. Have you heard anything from Johnny?" Cali asked, ignoring the question about her face. She wondered how come he didn't come visit her or she hadn't heard anything from him since she was in the hospital.

"To be honest, I don't know what happened to him. You know we don't speak like that." Delano hesitated on telling her the truth. He wasn't sure how Cali was going to respond to him killing her brother.

So, he decided not to tell her that he was the one behind pulling the trigger. Cali's tears began to fall as she began to assume the worst. This was not like her baby brother to just disappear. Although Johnny was a motherfucka, he still was her blood regardless of what he had done.

"Well you're more than welcome to come stay in my guest house for now. Kairo is gone with her family for the week and I'm sure she wouldn't mind you staying there," Delano offered. He felt sorry for her, watching the tears fall from her eyes.

"Are you sure?" Cali asked. "I don't want to be too much of a problem."

Delano shrugged his shoulders. He didn't see why Cali would be too much of a problem. By Kairo not mentioning Cali's involvement in the kidnapping, he thought everything was good between them. Had Kairo told him about Cali's involvement, she would have been dead because Delano would have killed her. So, she sat there in silence for the remainder of the ride, contemplating on her grand plan to kill Kairo.

Once Delano reached his residence, he pulled in front of a sub-outlet of his house, which had black and white trimming around the shutters of the windows, and tossed Cali a pair of keys. "Go ahead and get settled in. I will see you in few," Delano said, dropping Cali off in front of the guest house.

She walked inside her temporary home and sent a text message to Johnny to see if he would respond, but he didn't. *Hmm, that's weird*, she thought when the message came back green instead of blue. "I'll worry about that later," she said, throwing her phone back on the charger, going on a small tour of the house before coming to her room.

"Ahhh, I can shower at last, without having to get a sponge bath," Cali said as she began to take her clothes off. Delano had knocked twice on the main door and let himself in once he heard the shower get started. Soon as Cali was getting ready to step into the shower, Delano walked in catching her backside.

"Oh shit, my bad California. I didn't know you weren't in the shower yet," Delano said, walking into the bathroom dropping the towels on the floor and covering his eyes. He had seen Cali naked plenty times before from their previous flings, but he was trying to buckle down and be faithful to Kairo.

"It's ok, you've seen me naked before. Nothing much has changed except I gained a little more weight." Cali was now stopping in mid stroll to go pick up the towels Delano dropped. She bent down in front of him on purpose, hoping he would want to taste what he'd been missing.

"Uh, ok, California this is getting too awkward for me, so I'm going to go make a drink. You are more than welcomed to join me on my patio, but put some clothes on first." He turned and left out the bathroom.

Delano knew Cali was trying to seduce him, but he was no longer interested in her sexually. After he witnessed Kairo cheat on him yesterday, he swore to cut anything he had off with Cali. By this time, it was too little too late because Cali had already developed stronger feelings. Her feelings were so deep into him, she could swim in them.

CALI DRIED OFF, got dressed and joined a very drunk Delano outside for a drink on his patio. He was just sitting there drinking his Heineken gazing up at the stars in the sky. Cali poured her a glass of 1800 Silver Tequila and pulled a chair up beside him.

"I must admit, I am really impressed with your home you share with Kairo," she complimented.

"Oh, yea, well thanks!" Delano said as he sat up and adjusted in his chair.

"You know, after all these years, I'm still in love with you," Cali admitted. She moved closer and saw this was the perfect opportunity to approach Delano about her feelings.

"Listen Cali, what we had was fun, but the past is the past. You know I'm engaged to Kairo. We can't be doing that anymore," Delano responded carelessly.

"Really, why is that? Because you had no problem doing it with me before, so, why stop now?" Cali was now getting upset. Delano was playing roles all this time, now he wanted to switch up the tempo. She was not about to have that, so she stormed away to get the DNA papers. He needed to know about Malachi, so she was about to tell him. Cali got to her room and checked her phone to see if Johnny responded before sending another text, then she returned to the patio.

"Cali, I apologize, but can we not talk about this tonight?" Delano stammered. He was drunk off just the Heineken beer alone.

"Talk about what? Let's talk about the fact that when I was fourteen, I gave birth to OUR son?" Cali was now heated, pacing the patio back and forth as she tightly gripped those papers.

"Son?" Delano questioned. This was the first time of him hearing about a son, especially having one that young with Cali.

"Yes, motherfucka, that's right, a SON!" Cali yelled, watching Delano look dumbfounded. He didn't understand what drugs Cali was on, but he couldn't have had a son with her, at least that's what he thought.

"What, how is that even possible? We only did it once." Delano was confused.

"It only takes one time Delano, and I got pregnant the first time." Cali was still holding on to her papers.

"So, where the fuck is he now Cali?" he asked anxiously.

"He is here, just waiting on an invite from you, but you be on bullshit. One minute you tell me you love me and the next minute I'm just nothing to you anymore." Cali began walking closer to him slowly, step by step. Like a lioness coming to catch her prey, and in this case, Delano was her prey.

"You don't even know if he is mine or not. Your father was raping you too. So, how you are so sure he is my son?" Delano gave a low blow to Cali bringing up her past, but he did have a valid point. Cali knew for sure, that's why she had the papers to prove to him he was the father. She took DNA from him one day and got it tested, and the results came back 99.9%.

"Oh, I'm sure. Here, look for yourself," Cali said, slamming the papers in his hand. When Delano took the papers out of Cali's hand, his mouth opened wide. He couldn't utter a single word; he was just that broken.

11

THE TRUTH IS...

Delano just stood there speechless, without a single word escaping his mouth. Now the only thing that was on his mind was murder. He didn't even want to get tested. He knew they didn't have unprotected intercourse, but there were a lot of times they came close.

"SO, YOU'RE HIV POSITIVE?" Delano yelled at Cali. She then realized she had given him the wrong papers.

"What? That can't be right." Cali snatched the papers out Delano's hand, looking at the big words HIV POSITIVE written across the top along with her name.

"I can't believe this shit man." Delano scoffed with both of his hands in his face. "When were you going to tell me?"

"I swear, I was!" Cali screamed.

"SHUT YO' LYING ASS UP! BITCH, HOW LONG YOU KNEW YOU WERE HIV POSITIVE?" Delano cut into Cali, yelling at her. She didn't want to say another word. She was afraid of Delano, of what he was going to do next. So, she secretly sent a message.

"I'll just go." Cali got up and started walking towards the guest house.

"GO? GO WHERE BITCH? YOU'RE NOT LEAVING HERE

ALIVE IF I GOT TO KILL YOU MYSELF!" Delano was not having it, because he knew it was a possibility he was infected and that he infected Kairo as well. Although they were having intercourse with protection, they still had oral sex.

Delano and Cali were so caught up on finding out their status that they didn't know Kairo walked in the house. Kairo's father dropped her off because Delano wasn't answering his phone, so he just went on ahead and made that long trip to make sure his daughter got home. Once Kairo got in, she heard all the commotion out back, followed by Delano yelling at someone. So, Kairo had to go see what was going on and maybe get an answer to why Delano was not answering his phone.

"Please De—"

"Please what?" Kairo said, walking onto the patio. Delano was shocked. He wasn't expecting Kairo to be home. He looked at his phone and saw 24 missed calls from her.

"Oh shit, baby, I didn't know you were here." Delano sounded like he'd just been caught red handed with his pants down.

"DELANO, PPLLLLLEEEAAAASSSSEEEEE ! Enlighten me on what the fuck is going on here, because why the fuck is this backstab-bing ass bitch here?" Kairo asked. She knew she didn't see Cali in her back yard after this bitch was trying to kill her a month ago.

"You want to tell her, or shall I?" Cali challenged Delano, knowing he wasn't going to say anything.

"Bitch, was I talking to you?" Kairo drew her 9mm gun from her purse, pointing it at Cali's head.

"Kairo, we've been through this before. I think you know what I'm capable of." Cali had her hands up surrendering. Her heart was beating so rapidly, you could hear it beating out her chest. Kairo looked at both Delano and Cali, disgusted. She knew it would only be a matter of time before shit revealed itself.

"Baby, put the gun down and let's talk about this." Delano held both of his hands out, waving them in front of him. It was funny to Kairo, so she laughed. It was just yesterday he had the gun on her, now it was her with the gun towards him.

"Talk about what? You want to talk about the fact that we might all be in this bitch HIV positive?" Kairo overheard everything that Delano said because he was so loud. "Someone is not gone leave this bitch alive tonight, so who will it be? Eenny, meenie, miny, moe." *POW!!* Kairo waved the gun back and forth between Delano and Cali before shooting. The bullet ricocheted off the concrete balcony, grazing Delano's right thigh.

"AHHHHHHH! What the fuck! You're supposed to be on my side Kairo," Delano said, holding his thigh. Cali was still standing there plotting how she was going to get this gun out of Kairo's hand.

"Am I? Because you weren't on my side when you were just balls deep inside that poison bitch, were you?" Delano shook his head no. He couldn't even argue because he knew he was wrong. Kairo took a deep inhale before exhaling. She'd already been through a lot and they hadn't even made it to the altar yet. Looking back, Kairo's life wasn't filled with this much drama until Delano confessed his feelings. She might have come short on her bills, but she would have been better without him.

"Baby, I'm sorry. Please forgive me?"

"This is no ordinary love," Kairo responded, because she wasn't going to forgive Delano if she had HIV or not. She was going to walk away from everything, she wasn't going to marry this cheater.

"After you tried to humiliate me, you tried to kill me, now you're in my house fucking my man. What you got to say for yourself?"

Kairo laughed again, because it was just a month ago Cali was tough and had her chained to a chair. Now the tables were turned. It was Cali sitting in the chair with a gun pointed to her head. She had a lot of mouth but didn't know how to use those hands. If Cali knew how to defend herself then her face wouldn't be so badly disfigured.

"I have nothing to say," Cali murmured, looking off to the side knowing she was wrong.

"So, you have nothing to say about your actions?"

Cali shook her head, nope.

"Alright," Kairo said, holding her 9mm to Cali's head. She was about to blast Cali's brains everywhere until she kicked Kairo in the same calf Johnny shot her in. Kairo felt the pain shoot throughout her leg, but she didn't let that gun go.

"Bitch, I'm tired of your shit. I fucking hate you!" Cali said violently as she was pouncing on top of Kairo, tussling trying to get the gun. Delano ran to break up the two women as they were fighting like their lives depended on it.

"STTTOOOPPP IT!!!!" Delano tried pulling both women apart, but every time he had them separated, they would continue to fight. Kairo didn't have any hair for Cali to grip on so she dug her nails deep into Kairo's skin like she was Catwoman. Cali was fighting with all her might. She was trying her best to kill Kairo, but Kairo was the one with the gun. They continued to tussle, going back and forth before Kairo dropped the gun out her hand. Now all three of them tried reaching for that gun. Kairo tried to keep it from Cali, Cali tried to keep it from Kairo, and Delano wanted to keep it from them both.

However, Cali ended up reaching it first and tried to point it towards Kairo, but Kairo's strength was greater than hers and she forced Cali to point the gun downwards.

"Ahhh, let it go you bitchhhh!" Kairo yelled.

POW!

A gunshot rang through the night sky, and both Kairo and Cali stilled. Delano saw the blood spilling onto the ground on the patio and pushed Kairo off of Cali, making sure it wasn't Kairo that got shot.

"Ah, helppp meeee!" Cali said weakly, laying down reaching out for help. She was choking and gasping for air as she bled to death on their patio.

"No help from me, bitch!" *POW!* Kairo fired a shot into Cali's skull, taking her out her misery.

"Baby, what the fuck!!" Delano said, grabbing his head. He couldn't believe Kairo just murdered someone in their back yard.

"Help me get this bitch in the car," Kairo demanded as she took the curtains down out the dining room and wrapped Cali's body in them. Delano helped Kairo put Cali's body in the back of his Navigator truck. They both drove down to Detroit and let her body get shredded by the train on E Warren since it was low-key. Then they set the truck on fire so the police wouldn't be able to trace it back to them.

After watching the truck burn with Cali's body inside, they disposed whatever was left into the Detroit River.

"Hasta luego!" Kairo said as she dusted off her hands.

"Baby, we tell no one about this!" Delano said, calling them an Uber to get home.

"Yea, no finding out about our HIV status unless we're together!" Kairo suggested, and Delano agreed.

TRUST NO ONE

TWO WEEKS LATER...

K nock knock! Kairo and Delano awoke to the loud knocks on their bedroom door and the sunlight beaming in their eyes. Their new staff was still getting used to their new roles, so they didn't know not to knock on their door until after 10 am. Kairo glanced over at the clock and saw it was 9:20 am.

"Come in!" Kairo said, still yawning from being woken up so suddenly. She'd completed a shift at Beaumont and just got in at three am.

"I'm sorry, there is someone here requesting to see Mr. Harris," their new maid whose name was Shiloh said, holding onto the bedroom door. Kairo looked over at Delano, who went back to sleep and didn't flinch.

"Ok, I'll get it," Kairo said, huffing while rolling her eyes. She slipped on her royal blue silk robe and grabbed her 9mm off the table because they rarely get visitors unless it was family. She took her time walking down the stairs because she was tired still from that 12-hour shift she did last night.

When Kairo opened the door, a young man turned around smiling. Kairo pointed the gun directly at the young man's face. She didn't know if he came in peace or if he was a spy, she just automatically assumed he was a messenger. Delano came to the top of the stairs to see who it was, and told Kairo to lower her gun, to let the young man speak.

"Oh, I'm sorry, I didn't know I was a threat," the young man said with his hands up. He was just following the directions he had on a piece of paper that was mailed to him recently.

"State your business young man," Delano demanded, trying to speed the process up.

"I'm sorry, my name is Malachi and I'm looking for my father Delano Harris. My mother is California Jones," Malachi said, looking up at Delano who had some serious explaining to do. Kairo's bottom lip dropped.

"Oh, nah baby, you got the wrong house!" Kairo said, slamming the door in the young man's face.

"PLEASE MA'AM, I NEED TO SEE MY FATHER," Malachi said as he pounded hard on the door. Kairo turned towards Delano. This was some news to her ears.

"You got a fucking son with Cali?" Kairo asked, but Delano ignored her and came down to open the door. "Excuse me, I'm fucking talking to you!" Kairo's voice had gotten hostile. Delano didn't have anything to say, he just stepped aside and let Malachi in. Kairo wasn't too thrilled to find out about Cali and Delano sharing a past or a 14-year-old son together. "See, there you go hiding shit from me again!! What the fuck Delano?" Kairo said with an attitude. She was tired of being in the dark. She knew their relationship wasn't perfect, but she never kept any secrets from him. "Fuck this!" Kairo screamed before going on a rampage.

She went around the mansion destroying expensive furniture. She broke damn near every glass in the household except the windows. Delano nor their staff even stopped her, Delano just stood there and let Kairo express herself. He had insurance on all that shit she broke anyway. She went as far as pouring bleach on Delano's PS4, Xbox and his Wii's. They didn't even make Wii systems anymore, so he'd finally had enough after that.

"Ok, Kairo you are doing too much now," Delano said, but Kairo didn't give a damn, she kept going. Delano fired a bullet into the ceiling, which still didn't stop Kairo.

"Oh, nigga you want to shoot, I'ma shoot too!" Kairo said, reaching for her 9mm and shooting the glass out the windows. POW POW POW! The sounds of glass shattering and Kairo's 9mm echoed through the mansion. Malachi was appalled by Kairo's rage. He never meant to piss her off, all he wanted was to meet this notorious kingpin everyone kept talking about.

"KAIRO, STOP THIS SHIT RIGHT THE FUCK NOW!" Delano yelled with so much anger and frustration in his voice. He knew he was wrong for not telling Kairo about his alleged son with Cali, but really that would have made things worse. By this time, Kairo was done with her rampage after she broke a couple of dishes along the way to getting her car keys.

"Is there anything else I need to know?" Kairo stood in the foyer before leaving. Delano nodded his head no. "I'm going to my sister Asia's for a couple of hours. Figure this shit out before I get back." Kairo left abruptly, slamming the door behind her. The staff was upset, they had so much to clean after they'd just dusted the whole entire mansion from top to bottom.

"C'mon, let's go. We need to handle something," Delano said to Malachi stepping over the broken glass Kairo shattered during her rampage. Delano had never seen Malachi until today, so he needed to make sure this was his son. He did have a few resemblances to Delano but mainly Cali. "So how old are you kid?" Delano asked. He already knew how old Malachi was, he just wanted to make the ride as least as awkward as possible.

"I'm 14, going on 15 this month in January," Malachi replied as he was watching the snow fall slowly on the ground. The sunlight reflected off the snow while Delano drove smoothly over the salty streets. Delano paid close attention to Malachi's actions. He needed to know if he was also a traitor.

"How'd you find me?" Delano questioned. He wanted to know if he had any contact with Cali.

"My adoptive parents gave me a letter when I turned 14. I was supposed to read it once I turned 16. But if my biological mother died before I turned 16, then I would have to find you myself. Two weeks ago, I received a letter from Cali and she gave me a number to contact her," Malachi replied.

"Yea, I understand all that, but how did you find me at my house? I don't know your peoples." Delano pulled up in front of the Genetic Diagnoses building on Mack in Harper-wood. Malachi was careful not to give up his sources; he didn't want to snitch. "What's wrong, cat got your tongue?" Delano asked, parking his new Navigator in the rear end of the building.

"You know you're not that hard to find. I can't tell you my connection or how I found you and your address, I'm no snitch," Malachi protested. He was many things, auto thief, a small weed dealer, but he was no snitch. It was those exact words that Malachi spoke that let Delano know Malachi was no traitor. Both Delano and Malachi entered the building to take a genetic blood test. The nurses swabbed the insides of Delano's and Malachi's mouths and took blood samples before the test got started. As they were waiting for the results, Malachi wanted to learn more about his alleged father.

"So, where are you from?" Malachi asked, chewing on a tuna sandwich he'd just gotten from the vending machine. Delano was looking up at the TV that was posted in the top corner of the room. He was watching the news on channel 4, something he rarely did. "Hello, earth to Delano!" Malachi said, waving his hands in Delano's eye view.

"I heard you kid. I'm from here, Detroit, and can you excuse me really quick?" Delano responded, stepping away to dial Kairo's number, but he got voicemail. Kairo, I need you at the house by the time I get home, I love you." Delano left Kairo a message and returned to the lobby just in time to get his results.

"It's turns out you are 99.9% Malachi's father Mr. Harris, congratulations," the nurse said, reading Delano and Malachi's results. Delano was happy he had a son. Malachi was relieved, but he needed to come clean about his situation.

"Now that we know the truth, what do we do next?" Malachi asked. He wanted to get to know his father as much as possible. All his life Malachi was in and out of adoptive families' homes, and this was his chance to have at least one of his parents be a part of his life.

"I'll tell you what," Delano paused, "what time you got to be home?" Delano asked.

"To be honest, I don't have a home. I live in a group home called Don Bosco off Collingwood and Petoskey on the Westside," Malachi replied, ashamed. Delano was familiar with the home. It was across the Boy's and Girl's Club.

"Don't be ashamed my son, I know exactly where that is. From now on, you're going to move in with me and your soon-to-be step-mother," Delano said, wrapping his arms around his son. He knew Kairo would be upset, but that was his son. He wasn't gone let his seed just be in the streets.

Delano took Malachi shopping for a new wardrobe and purchased him a brand-new yellow Chevy Camaro. He got all the necessities Malachi needed to feel comfortable living with him. Delano even had his men expedite the paperwork, changing Malachi's last name to Harris.

Leaving the mall, Delano looked down at his phone and realized the time was now 6 pm and this was not like Kairo to go all day without speaking to him. No matter how mad Kairo was at Delano she still made sure to check in. Delano had a gut feeling something was wrong, so he tried calling her a few times and got her voicemail. He tried tracking her, but that didn't work if her phone was dead. Something was not right, and Delano knew it wasn't. He and Malachi loaded their bags into the truck and pulled off. Delano kept dialing Kairo, but now her shit wasn't even ringing anymore.

He thought to stop by her sister Asia's, but he didn't want to just drop by without calling first. So, he dialed Asia on speed dial, and she told him Kairo left to go home an hour ago. This made Delano stop worrying and think maybe she went to sleep, but he would never know until he got home. Delano sped home doing over 100 mph to get to New Baltimore, MI.

Upon arrival, he noticed Kairo's Range was out front, parked next to a black Charger. Delano grabbed his heat from the glove compartment. "Son, no matter what happens, stay in the car," Delano warned Malachi before getting out the truck. He crept up on his own porch, and every single light was off, the only light he had was the moonlight. He noticed the door to his foyer was already ajar and pushed the door open completely, flicking on the lights. In front of him sat Kairo tied to a chair with tape over her mouth. Soon as he was about to run towards her, he felt a gun on his back.

"NAH, partner, not so fucking fast!" a familiar voice said, as he pushed the gun further in Delano's back ushering him to move. As he was walking slowly towards Kairo, Delano thought he could outsmart the man who had the gun. Soon as he turned a bullet ripped right through Delano's shoulder.

"AAAAAAGGGGHHHHH!" Delano screamed as he felt the bullet pierce his right shoulder. He fell to the floor, looking up as if he saw a ghost when he saw Johnny's face. Delano thought he was dead. He watched him fall to the ground after he shot him multiple times. Everyone thought he was dead, but he still survived because he had on a bulletproof vest. He got shot twice but the rest the vest caught.

"Remember me, nigga?" Johnny said, stepping on Delano's bloody shoulder.

"Alright Johnny, play nice. We need the nigga alive to find your sister," Johnny Sr. said, walking into the living room. He was released early due to good behavior, and now he was back looking for Cali. Johnny sat Delano up and tied him to the chair just like Kairo was.

"Delano, I find it clever of you and this bitch here you call your fiancée to get rid of my daughter after she comes clean to you about my grandson Malachi," Johnny Sr. said, blowing smoke into his face.

"Man, I don't know what the fuck you are talking about!" Delano yelled at Johnny Sr. He knew exactly what happened. It had been two weeks since Delano and Kairo killed Cali, but to Johnny Sr. and Johnny, she was considered missing. The last time they heard from her was when she gave them the address to Delano's residence. They were to seek her only if they hadn't heard from her. So, here they were in the living room.

"I now have a missing daughter, Delano, and I have a feeling you

125

might have killed her," Johnny Sr implied. Although he was certainly right, he would never believe that until he recovered her bones.

"I haven't seen shit!" Delano yelled.

"Nigga don't talk to my dad like that." Johnny punched Delano in the rib cage just as he did to him.

"Bitch, we know about your faggot ass. You're probably the reason Cali had HIV!" Delano retorted. Johnny Sr and Johnny were both caught by surprise.

"What the fuck he just say?" Johnny Sr. asked. He knew his son better not had liked dick. They both couldn't like the same thing.

"No, hold on." Johnny held his hand up at his father. "What the fuck you just say nigga?" Johnny asked again.

"I said, bitch-you-a-fag," Delano said slowly so the words could register in Johnny's head, upsetting him.

He took the gun and aimed it at Kairo's head. *POW! POW! POW!*

- To be Continued

A NOTE FROM THE AUTHOR

Hello Love Bugs!!!

I hope you have enjoyed reading the story just as much as I did writing it. This is my very first novel, so I wanted to you to be a part of this experience. I want to encourage you to follow your dream, no matter what may come up against you. In life we go through many trials, some greater than others, but no matter what, stick in there. You must achieve what YOU believe in. Stay tuned friends, pt 2 is coming soon.

Until next time, chao.

ABOUT THE AUTHOR

April Nicole Marie, is a loving, devoted mother who was born and raised in the city of Detroit better known as the "Motor City." She began her writing career at the age of 13, traveling and winning oratorical speeches around the city.

Inspired by her favorite Authoress "Zane" she began to write her own erotica short stories in high school, sharing them amongst her class mates. April graduated from M. L. King High school in 2012, and later attended Davenport University majoring in Business Administration. Now April is currently employed as a Credit Specialist at a well-known corporation, and plan on pursuing her writing career full time. If you ever want drama, entertainment, and a thrill look no further. She is here to bring that heat. You will constantly be at the edge of your seat wanting to know what's going to happen next.

Stay Connected:
Follow me on Facebook "April Nicole's Erotic Short Stories," or if you have any questions or suggestions please email me at
aprilnicolemarie@gmail.com.

f

9 781648 400001